Praise for *Love and Death on Long Island*

"Heartrending. Adair's realization of his chief character seems faultless. . . . The book is a startlingly precise miniature."—*The Evening Standard* (London)

"Romantic and ruminative yet always precise, a comedy of longing propelled by a strong current of satirical observation. . . . De'Ath may be a creep, but he's also a true hero."—David Denby, *New York* (on the film)

"Slyly erotic, erudite. . . . A beautifully executed pastiche."—*Independent on Sunday* (UK)

"Beautifully crafted. . . . It's the smooth flow of the writing and the close attention to detail which make it such a delightful book to read. A perfectly faceted gem."—*Time Out* (UK)

"A delicious comedy."—*Time*

GILBERT ADAIR

Love and Death
on Long Island

GROVE PRESS
New York

First published in Great Britain in 1990
by William Heinemann Ltd.
Published simultaneously in Canada
Printed in the United States of America

FIRST AMERICAN EDITION

Library of Congress Cataloging-in-Publication Data

Adair, Gilbert.
Love and death on Long Island / Gilbert Adair.
p.   cm.
ISBN 0-8021-3592-7
I. Title.
PR6051.D287L68   1998
823'.914—dc21   98-22274

Grove Press
841 Broadway
New York, NY 10003

98 99 00 01 10 9 8 7 6 5 4 3 2 1

to Meredith Brody,
for being there

I do not know why I should have come to so abrupt a halt in the middle of the broad pavement of the street along which I had been walking an instant before with, to all outward appearance, not a care in the world. Conveniently, or perhaps this it was which caused me to stop there rather than elsewhere, the first thing I noticed as I stared about me in bafflement was a street sign attached to a low brick garden wall. It read 'Fitzjohn's Avenue'. For the moment I felt quite disoriented, I was incapable of deciding whether or not I ought to register some little amazement at the fact that I was still in Hampstead, still at a sensible distance from home instead of halfway across London or dear knows where. Evidently I had stepped out at my own garden gate and, for one reason or another, a reason that may have had nothing in common with reason in any more abstract sense, had chosen not to stroll upwards towards the Heath as was my customary practice. Instead, I must have taken Frognal Rise and by some circuitous route of which I had only the very vaguest recollection – possibly by Church Row? – now found myself moving out of Hampstead altogether. I had left home, it's true, with no specific destination in mind, just an enervated conviction that I 'had to get out', and it was no doubt when I reached that stretch of Fitzjohn's Avenue where it might be said to gather speed, as it were, like a current about to plunge headlong into the ocean of the metropolis that lies beneath it, and when I knew, if only 'unconsciously', that I had been following a longer and straighter path than was feasible within the snug, verdant maze of Hampstead proper, with all its lamplit 'crescents' and 'rises' and 'rows', that an obscure territorial mechanism cautioned me to stop and take stock.

The pavements on both sides of the street were free of pedestrians and no traffic seemed to be travelling in either direction. Fitzjohn's Avenue is almost entirely residential, bordered by large and pleasant if sometimes slightly uncommunicative private houses with rambling and even derelict front gardens and red-brick walls high enough to hide from the undesired gaze of a passer-by all but their rooftops or low enough to expose the whole façade from driveway to chimney pots or else suddenly giving way to a slatted, charred-looking sort of fencing. Here and there, too, one passes a church, an orphanage or a convent school. But I had observed none of these, for as I descended the avenue at an uncommonly lively tread my observations had all been of a seethingly internal order. Only now did I view the need to consider my immediate surroundings as an imperative one.

The house in front of which I happened to be standing, and on whose garden wall was affixed the signpost that had caught my eye, differed from its neighbours in appearing tolerably new, certainly newly repainted; that combined with a vague Dutch or pseudo-Dutch style of architecture and a very unrambling rock garden lent it a queerly miniaturised look. Emphasising its toylike aspect was the number-sign nailed on to the gate. This had been contrived out of a single piece of varnished wood which reminded me of some old-fashioned painter's palette (although the two shapes were in fact quite dissimilar) and on which was carved, in letters not numbers, *Forty-Three A*. There was, as I could not help thinking, something most definitely un-Hampstead in such arch and suburban artfulness.

It was, however, the garden itself to which my attention was drawn. It was laid out, naïvely symmetrically, with plants in pots and flowers in flowerbeds, to practically none of which I, a writer so often praised for my descriptive powers, could have put a name. But pride of place had been given by the house's occupiers to, of all improbable trees, a palm.

The intention had doubtless been to contribute an inkling of exoticism to the dull, housebroken leafiness of NW3, to make of this poor solitary palm tree a synecdoche and symbol of the light and warmth and colour of which the British quotidian round is so starved. Yet its effect on me, as an uneasiness of spirit invested the matter with an intensity I could not explain, was completely the reverse. The presence of the palm, set to very moot advantage by a meandering string of little white pebbles that looped around its base and an arrangement of turquoise-and-yellow flowers so orderly it might have served as a pattern on a woman's blouse, only underscored how alien it was to its setting. It transported me no further southwards, nowhere more exotic or alluring, than Torquay, that insipid jewel of the 'English Riviera' – Torquay of the palm-skirted putting greens and promenades. Its having been uprooted in this manner filled me with the same distaste and pity as would an elephant trained to stand up on its hind legs in a circus act.

Really, it was an inoffensive enough thing to encounter

3

on a Hampstead lawn, and no one else would have afforded it more than a glance. But it was there that I chanced to stop and, if not this, then something else would have allowed me to objectify my exasperation with the world and its ineradicable mediocrity, to pronounce, not precisely aloud, the anathema I had been harbouring inside of me since I left home: 'All journalists be damned to Hell!'

I was born in the year of grace 193– and as a writer had been – somewhat to the surprise of my contemporaries at Cambridge, who had expected the greatest things of me – what is generally called a late developer. Orphaned during my final year, and made wealthy by the tragedy, I was of course without the incentive of any pressing material need to commit myself to literary expression of whatever variety or depth and, until the latter sixties, had brought out just a short, indifferently published study of the sixteenth-century Mannerist school of painting – the kind of thing that was no more and perhaps even a trifle less than might have been looked for in someone of such obvious brilliance. In every other respect, that period of my life remained as sketchy and enigmatic to those with whom I had formed close friendships at university, and there were few enough of them, as it did to the scarcely more numerous readers and critics and fellow writers (for if anyone deserved the ungrateful epithet of 'writer's writer', it was I) who discovered what they judged to be talent of a quite extraordinary stamp in the series of four novels I wrote in swift succession from 1969 to the middle of the next decade.

These four novels – which were frequently referred to, to my intense annoyance, as a tetralogy – shared the theme of sacrifice, a theme to which their author seemed to be ascribing an explicitly religious or at the very least otherworldly significance. In spite of that, they had conventionally been read (especially in France, where my stock was higher than in my native country and my work had been compared to Blanchot's) as allegories of the quasi-sacrificial act of writing itself and the correlative condition of perpetual and agonising incertitude that it induces in the writer. Of the four individual sacrifices chronicled in the novels not one is shown to have been justified.

Fastidiously textured, unlyrical and superficially uneventful save for the pivotal act, curiously timeless in atmosphere despite the occasional and, as some believed, rather intrusive allusion to the Holocaust, they were of personal inspiration only in the paradoxical sense that the equivocal convulsions of self-abnegation which made up their subject matter appeared to be mirroring, in what the French term a *mise en abyme*, my own self-effacing attitude to language as the externalisation of an interiority. (Lately, for example, one of my American exegetes had created something of a minor sensation in academic circles by demonstrating that not once in the entire corpus of my published writings, fictional and non-fictional, and even unto those extremely rare exchanges of dialogue that speckled my fiction, had I had recourse to the first person singular: in short, even when assuming the voice of one of my protagonists, I had never brought myself to say 'I' in print.) At any rate, they had enjoyed no commercial success whatsoever. In England, where an unprecedented shift in social mores had ended with the relaxing of censorship, their cold, demure narratives could not have seemed less of their own time. Even across the Channel their total absence of direct political engagement or ideological underlay would repel many a potential admirer.

The situation remained unaltered throughout the following ten years. I ceased to write – or, more exactly, to publish – and at the same time I wholly ceased to make my never very frequent and frankly merely dutiful attendances at theatrical first nights and private views. It was heard that I had married, that my wife was considerably older than I and without connections in the world of literature, and that I had more or less retreated to my house in Hampstead. As the years passed this or that was heard, that I had been travelling, that my only real friends, whom I sporadically visited, were a small coterie of Cambridge dons, that my wife had died – in truth, though, the world, with its own affairs to attend to, paid next to no attention to my doings. Like more writers than most people ever suppose, I had absolutely no public life, and both the world and I appeared to prefer it that way.

Yet these four novels of mine refused conclusively to go away. Little by little, in part because of intrinsic qualities that were great and durable enough to survive any lengthy period of neglect, in part because the passions of the two previous decades had quite cooled down, and in most part because of the subtle but indisputable nimbus of rarefaction that enhaloed my work, the cachet that will ever be attached to an artist fallen silent in his prime and whose silence fascinates as an impertinent shunning of the world and the blandishments it holds out to those it deigns to regard as gifted, I returned to fashion. I was not, even then, widely read. No commuter ever selected one of my novels as the ideal 'read' for a tedious journey by rail. But they were reissued in paperback form, as Modern Classics no less, and had appended to them introductions by some of the younger novelists – introductions that I thought moronic but was willing to accept as the price I had to pay to gain a new readership, an opportunity to which I was more alert than might have been predicted. There meanwhile came my way so many requests for translation rights that I had to call on the services of an agent. For the first time in my life I was making money out of my books.

Concurrently with this (all very relative) rise to celebrity, I started writing again. Not fiction – that period seemed to have reached an end – but works that were not easily definable offhand, libraries tending to catalogue them either under Philosophy or Art Criticism. The most esteemed of these had been a history of angels – which is to say, a history of the representation of angels in all the arts but particularly in painting. Into the prose of this long essay – whose premise, crudely put, was that only by aspiration to and concourse with some form of the super-natural (a word I invariably hyphenate) was the artist able to create out of the humility that is, or should be, his natural state and essence – there had come a sweetness of descriptive colouring and a near-morbid refinement of expression for which nothing else I had written would have prepared the reader: more than one critic approvingly cited Pater's *The Renaissance*. It was, to be sure, no less 'dated' in conception and style than my earlier volumes. But the period in which it was published was infected by that febrile eclecticism of taste that is peculiar to every *fin de siècle* and had no difficulty accommodating what it interpreted as a wilful and even 'postmodern' archaism on my part. Its reception was such, in consequence, that my latest book could lay claim to rather more than the tepid aura of anticipation that had always been my lot.

To this work I had given the title *The Gentrification of the Void*. It was a title that procured me a certain secret euphoria – the more so as I had arrived at it almost by chance since the one I had previously intended to use and which now struck me as pompous and overdetermined, *The Death of the Future*, had initially been rejected only because of what would have been the infelicitous proximity on the book's jacket of the word 'death' with my own absurd surname. Coincidentally, the work itself, due to be published imminently, was a reflection on precisely the phenomenon of postmodernism and was already attracting a degree of pre-publication curiosity by virtue of its modish subject matter. And even if anyone at all conversant with the hauteur and austerity of my thought would know that such a book must bear scant resemblance to the racy, jargon-strewn productions that the postmodern movement had already inspired, the fashionableness of my theme in conjunction with the revived prestige of my name was so potent that, a few weeks before taking that walk down Fitzjohn's Avenue, I had been rung up by my agent with the news that a certain expensive, trend-setting magazine for men (of which I had never heard) was interested in buying the serialisation rights.

For my agent the call had been made out of duty. But, to his astonishment, I consented to the request. Why, I could scarcely have said. Money was not a primary consideration – though, as I told myself, I knew of no strong reason for refusing it. But such a sale would, above all, afford me almost mischievous gratification at the thought of how dismayed the magazine's editor would be when he received a proof copy and discovered that what he had purchased could not be further removed from all those horribly trumped-up articles, riddled with clichés as with cancerous cells, on the supposed post-modern properties of television advertisements and record sleeves and neo-classical insurance offices in the City, articles that I had felt obliged to read before starting my own essay. I had never sought easy acclaim and did not resent in the least having never attained it. But I would have been less than human were I not capable of taking a mildly gleeful pleasure in being offered the chance of wrongfooting that world which I so despised – and also of making a not inconsiderable sum of money.

I did not have very long to wait for my worst suspicions to be confirmed. A week or so after a proof of my book had been sent to the magazine in question, its features editor telephoned me to ask in a languorously incurious voice whether I would be so good as to suggest a passage suitable for extraction. I was polite and quite unforthcoming. Perhaps, I answered drily, if he were actually to read the book instead of, as had plainly been the case, just leafing through it with a solicitously professional eye, he might be capable of arriving at a decision without the author's assistance. Apparently unashamed by this rebuke to his competence – a traditional one for such an exchange, after all, and which he had no doubt heard before – the editor languidly mumbled something about having not wanted to misrepresent my thesis then all but hung up on me.

I placed the receiver down with a smile. The first round had gone to me. What did it matter which passage they chose for publication? No one would read it – or anyway finish it. And I had been able to prove that the world still boasted a small cluster of souls, poet-spokesmen, mandarins – yes, unrepentantly so! – who had not capitulated to the debased values of a society for which art was a mere commodity, as marketable and reproducible as another, a society in which, as I liked to say to my Cambridge friends, in one of the very rare witticisms that had ever been attributed to me, writers did not write, they processed words.

From that point onwards I should have forgotten all about the incident had not the same languid young man telephoned again a few days later, this time with the suggestion that only if accompanied by a personal interview with its author could the extract be (here, the features editor momentarily racked his brains before hitting on the *mot juste*) contextualised.

With a hint of tartness in my voice I replied that I never gave interviews. The editor persisted. Ignorant, however, of his interlocutor both as an artist and as a private individual, he at first botched his chance. His pitifully vulgar endeavours to flatter me fell so far wide of the mark they only strengthened me in my resolve. The conversation sputtered on thus for several minutes with my being barely able to fit a word in edgeways but none the less determined to draw the line at granting an interview; until the editor, as though in acknowledgement of the inevitable outcome and ceasing to feel too concerned with the poor impression he was about to leave on the man whose vanity he had been so actively caressing, delivered himself of a curt comment on writers who take the concentration camps for their theme (a coarse perversion of the generally understated way in which the memory of the Holocaust had been interpolated into my novels) and then decline to emerge from their secure and soundproofed ivory towers in NW3.

The reproach was no less clumsily phrased and philistine than the preceding flattery had been, but to an extent that the editor could not realise I was stung by the words 'ivory tower'. I had, as I have already intimated, neither regret nor nostalgia for the great humming world of business and letters and the wheels and deals by which it turns. Yet, equally so, I had travelled more in that world, further afield, too, than my detractors suspected, and the notion that I lived in an ivory tower struck me as most offensive and unjust. A few months back, when that American academic had brought out his paper on the first person singular that was so famously missing in my work, it distressed me more than I cared to admit (for I myself had remained unaware of such a compulsion). It incited me to wonder whether, on an incomparably more exalted plane, the artist in me did not resemble the sort of poor devil obliged to consult his doctor on the matter of a sordid physical affliction and to pretend shamefacedly to speak on behalf of some imaginary third party; to wonder, indeed, whether I might not accurately ascribe to pride, and to pride alone, the fact that I had sought so airless and inaccessible a path to self-fruition.

Immediately cutting through the editor's incoherent prattle with a weary 'Oh very well, yes', I stated that I would agree to be interviewed, but for no longer than an hour and at the hour of my choice – in my own house – on the following Sunday afternoon. This last proviso represented my sole remaining concession to a quite undiminished hostility towards the magazine and all its works. By fixing on a Sunday, for me a day that dawned no differently from any other, it had been my puerile intention simply to blight the weekend of some as yet unsuspecting journalist.

During the next three days – the conversation had taken place on a Thursday – I found my attention obstinately, distractingly, straying to the interview (the first I had ever submitted to in my career) and what my expectations of it ought reasonably to be. Would my interviewer, whose name had meant nothing to me, be just as unsavoury an individual as his superior? Would he even have read the book? Or, on the contrary, would he turn out to be surprisingly intelligent and well informed, as somewhere in my mind, with an obscure stirring of premature and rather paradoxical resentment, I started to think might be the case? In fact I prepared myself for wellnigh every eventuality save the one which did come to pass. The journalist stood me up.

At the exact hour of the appointment, three o'clock, I was in my study, sitting at a spacious writing desk by the half-open window and irritably scanning the *Telegraph*, over the top of whose pages I would glance up at the square marble-framed dial of the clock on the mantelpiece. A half-hour later, now positively quaking with fury (more especially as, it being a Sunday, I could not even ring up the editor to announce that such professional irresponsibility had forced me to call the interview off), I found I was unable to remain calm for more than ten or twenty seconds at a time. Then, when yet another three-quarters of an hour had elapsed (for I was still rational enough to allow for an initial misunderstanding in the hour arranged for the interview), and my wrath was fuelled by the now completely irrational conviction that the abortive rendezvous had been a trick deliberately perpetrated on me by the magazine's features editor, that I in short had been the wrongfooted one, I brusquely cast aside the newspaper I held in my hand, left the study, gathered up an overcoat and woollen scarf and, stepping into the cheerless damp air of a Sunday afternoon in early autumn, began that agitated and directionless stroll that would ultimately lead me, almost as though my very willpower had been paralysed, to no. 43A Fitzjohn's Avenue.

Nearby, a church bell had just chimed five times, and in the distance there was a wheezing, faint and ethereal, of what sounded like bagpipes. Having had my fill of the lonely palm tree, I was only now made aware that my own solitude was less absolute than I had supposed. There was no more traffic than before along the roadway itself. But a little further down the street, on the pavement opposite, a man in a drab fawn raincoat stood talking into a cellular telephone, quite alone and unabashed, as though he were enclosed by the traditional glass-walled booth. On my own side of the street, a young couple, most likely out on a routine, time-honoured Sunday afternoon walk, idly advanced towards me. They were preceded by a child, a three- or four-year-old of, from where I was standing, indeterminate gender, secured to its mother by a miniature lead and harness that fitted across its body. Just as I happened to look up in their direction the scampering child took a tumble and fell down hard on the pavement. For a moment or two, in anguish, it examined the two little scraped palms of its upturned hands; and at that stage of the crisis there still seemed a chance of warding off the cloudburst. Even so far away, however, I could already see the little one's innocent brow darken (as though the message that it had been hurt was at last reaching its brain) and its features suddenly crumple up. The tap had been opened, the squall could not now be long delayed and it wanted only that strange, childlike stay of execution, that instant of poised and expectant suspension, tempting one to conjecture that a child's tears must first travel along a tiny pipeline, for a loud howl to burst forth from the depths of its being.

Now the palm tree, now this infant's fall, the course of which I had tracked with a dry, detached sort of interest: I decided it was time to resume my walk and, if possible, to start getting some enjoyment out of it. I passed the young couple as the child was being comforted, her two palms (I could now observe that it was a little girl) being kissed in turn by her father, and I permitted myself a sympathetic smile and attempted a slightly self-conscious tut-tutting noise with my tongue. I also passed, without manifesting any especial curiosity, the man in the fawn raincoat who was still speaking into his queerly shaped telephone on the other side of the street. I passed others out strolling, more and more of them, for Fitzjohn's Avenue had meanwhile changed its name and become less residential, less conspicuously the reserve of a solid middle class. I noticed newsagents and launderettes and Chinese restaurants, and stopped to peer with lazy inquisitiveness into the window of a lone bookshop, which had been given over exclusively to devotional tracts by some rather dubious Indian and Tibetan mystics. And all the while, gnawing away at my peace of mind, there was the interview and the journalist who had failed to appear and the realisation that if I had always refused interviews in the past – over the years there had come odd, irregular requests – it was with the intention, one day, of granting The Interview, the 'unique, exclusive interview', as I fancied the journal in question would announce it, in which, lofty yet unpresumptuous, remote yet with a sly, sideways candour, eloquent yet never less than approachably human, I would finally, at a period when my reputation had nothing more either to gain or lose, unburden myself of the secrets of my productive energy. Instead of which, here I was, tramping the streets like a jilted lover!

Walking on thus – not at a heightened pace, as it may deceptively have seemed to me, but at the same speed as before, it being those now more numerous pedestrians crossing my path who left me with the impression of moving appreciably more briskly, the way a motionless train will be endowed with illusory movement by an adjacent one slowly edging out of the station – I found myself at a forked intersection and began to wonder whether I should think of retracing my steps or go on until I had outgrown my childish ill humour. But the decision was almost immediately made for me. As I stood irresolutely rooted to the spot it started to rain. A minute or so later the gutters were running freely, raindrops were skittering off the pavement at my feet and my fellow strollers had drawn mackintoshes up over their heads and were scrambling for cover.

It so happened that I was standing in front of a cinema. It was one of those vast *lumpen* pleasure palaces, now somewhat the worse for wear, peeling and unappealing, as you might say, that had been erected in the earliest postwar years to satisfy the cravings of a populace starved of myth and glamour, of fantasy and wit, and only waiting to capitulate to the easy, whorish and irresistible charms of that oblong swathe of alternative reality, the so-called silver screen. How many simple hearts had once quickened at the prospect of its scarlet-and-gold jewel box of an auditorium, its every single nook and cranny an encrustation of gaudy decorative frostwork, bas-reliefs and arabesques, Little Egypt friezes and Chinatown chinoiserie? And wouldn't those same hearts beat faster still at the instant the lights dimmed, the ruched curtains parted and the entire auditorium, orchestra stalls and balconies alike, gazed as raptly into the screen as a crescent of doting relatives into a newborn's cot? Isn't it Goethe who writes somewhere of the city of Rome as being inhabited by two distinct but harmoniously reconciled citizenries: the Roman people itself but also that noble minority of classical statues alongside which it unheedingly goes about its business? In England's cities, too, generation upon generation lived alongside their own 'ennobling' statuary – the statuary, here, of a world of screen-shadows – to whose fulgent and ingratiating presence they were long in unrepentant thrall. Alas, though, whatever used to be their cheap grandeur, these statues are now almost as ancient and superannuated as Goethe's; and the museums in which they were housed, like this cinema halfway between Hampstead and St. John's Wood, with its streaky, slablike concrete walls and scratched, discoloured paint, its forlornness of urban disuse and disrepair, only testify to their irreversible fall from grace.

For me, in any case, the massive overhang of its broad marquee provided merely a roof under which, uncramped, I could shelter for a minute or two, this picture palace's foyer having been designed in full and confident expectation of the kind of milling, good-natured throng that had long since abandoned it. As the rain was beginning now to beat down so heavily that the pavement looked as though it were receiving so many stabbing pains to the chest, I quickly stepped underneath and, shaking out the collar of my overcoat in the orthodox style, morosely stared at the streaming thoroughfare in front of me.

I had never partaken of the joyous simplicity of filmgoing – in fact, improbable as it must sound, I had been to the cinema not more than a dozen times in my life, in the most diverse and unpromising circumstances. I could remember seeing, for example, in the slightly bibulous company of two Cambridge acquaintances, a bad, recklessly abbreviated *Hamlet* with Olivier; and once with my wife, on a shopping excursion to the West

End, an idiotic Hollywood comedy, which someone or other had recommended, about a lascivious Californian hairdresser, a sort of odious ambulant phallus, in the throes of self-revelation. It was after that film that I vowed I would never visit a cinema again, and I never did. Nor had any film producer ever made enquiries as to the possibility of adapting one of my novels. If one had so enquired, then, founding my judgment upon that *Hamlet* and that hairdresser and upon not much else, I should have had the extreme pleasure, once more, of saying no.

Saying no, I thought, that has always been my forte, and no wonder, given that the stupidity of the world is rivalled only by its ugliness. And just at that moment I fancy a rather ugly, sarcastic little grin disfigured the lower half of my face as it suddenly struck me that this matter of the interview with which I was so preoccupied was after all by no means ended; that the unaccountable failure of my interviewer to make an appearance could hardly by itself close the chapter; and that, when the features editor of that deplorable self-styled 'magazine for men' telephoned me, as surely he would, to apologise for having inconvenienced me unnecessarily, and also no doubt to propose setting an alternative date, then, released as I would be from the need to respect any of the professional or even the simple human courtesies, I would seize the opportunity of letting him know precisely what I thought of him.

So delightful was the prospect of revenge that for the first time since walking out that day, and despite an awareness that my heart was beating a trifle too fast, I felt relatively at peace with myself. I drew a cigarette from my battered silver case and lit it. It was raining quite as violently as ever. Unless a cab were to chance to pass, an unlikely eventuality, I could not think of going home as yet. I blew the cigarette smoke out through my nostrils, tilting my head backwards as I tend to do, in an exquisitely refined parody of equine breathing or snorting. At the half-dozen others who like me had taken cover under the cinema's marquee, and were now huddled together in a semi-circle as though feeling that circumstances had obliged them to introduce themselves, I extended a brief, unobservant and unrequited glance and almost at once gazed away again. Then my eyes rested at last, merely for want of anything more stimulating to turn to, on the central buttress of the marquee, a sturdy four-square column that also served, by means of a display cabinet of seven or eight still photographs, to advertise the current programme.

The film was evidently a period piece, a prettified evocation, from the costumes shown in the stills, of that Edwardian era that constitutes one of the supreme pathetico-nostalgic Arcadias of the popular English imagination. In the first photograph to catch my attention a virginal young woman in a white dress and holding a white parasol was to be seen, escorted by a shirt-sleeved youth, wading through a meadow knee-high in unkempt, reedlike grasses and flowers. In another the same young woman, in more sombre clothes, was striking a fugitive attitude amid the statuary of what was unmistakably the piazza Signoria in Florence. A third represented a group of people of various ages in the shady and over-furnished interior of what I already knew or half-knew, by some form of intimate conviction, to be a Florentine boarding house, a *pensione*.

I had of course not seen the film. I recognised none of the actors. Yet somewhere inside my head, as a shivering thing unexplained by my intellect but quite real to my senses, I felt obscurely familiar with these characters and the settings in which they moved. Before even I read the film's title, inscribed as it was on a white underline bordering each of the stills, I knew that it was an adaptation of a novel by Forster, one far from being my own personal favourite but of which I had spoken at length to the ageing author himself, who had befriended me at Cambridge and whose protégé to a certain extent I had become. (I say to a certain extent, for it was a privilege I only gradually discovered I had been sharing with other young undergraduates of similar promise.)

I bent over to look more attentively at the stills. The film appeared surprisingly faithful to at least the textures and trappings of the book upon which it was based: scene after scene, character after character, I contrived to identify without any great problem and indeed with something very nearly approaching a pleasurable *frisson*.

The rain, driven off course by a high, blustery wind, so that I had to withdraw ever further into the foyer, showed no sign of letting up. Slate-blue in the gathering dusk, the street presented a singularly uninviting perspective. It occurred to me that, even if I did succeed in returning home without getting soaked through, though God knew how, what awaited me there was a miserable supper of cold cuts, by now probably curling at the edges, which my housekeeper (who didn't 'do' for me on a Sunday) would have left sandwiched between a couple of plates on my kitchen table. And so it was that, feeling just a trifle light-headed, rather like a schoolboy playing truant, I decided to go in and watch the film. I would see this adaptation of my mentor's novel, I would fairly cheerfully relax a lifetime vow, then treat myself, *une fois n'est pas coutume*, to dinner in a small French restaurant in Hampstead where my wife and I had oftentimes eaten together. Now that the whole mortifying business was being miraculously transformed into an amusing self-indulgence, I little cared whether the performance was halfway through or nearly at an end; however, it so fell out that it was timed to start in just under ten minutes.

When I entered the cinema, my heart sinking a little at the foyer's tawdry appointments, its smoky, wing-shaped light fittings and its carpeting so threadbare that the company logo which had been woven into it would have been legible only to those who knew exactly what they were looking at, it took me a while to locate the box office, which also served as a refreshment stand and was stocked with every type of confectionery, with popcorn machines and a soft-drink dispenser giving off a glow of such lustrous intensity as only chemistry has the secret. The cashier, a tiny, fat Filipina with a delicate bone structure, whose open palm was already thrust at me before I had time enough to reach for my wallet, took the crumpled note I handed her, drew forth a ticket, tore it in half, handed one half back to me and rammed some change home into my own outstretched palm, all in a single arc of unblinking indolence. I stared at her for a moment but at first said nothing. Then, when I began to ask, 'Where . . .?', she cocked her plump little head in the very vaguest of directions – the auditorium was somewhere behind me, was all I could gather – and turned at once to whatever it was under the counter, a book, a magazine, possibly a half-knitted jumper, that the banal routine of selling a ticket had come to interrupt.

There were three doors on the far side of the foyer; they were unmarked, yet they also appeared to be signalling 'Keep Out'. So, instead, I climbed a wide central stairway which led to a gallery lined with signed portraits of waxily personable male film stars – the signature had been scrawled on each of these portraits at such an angle it seemed as though the signatory were wearing it on his lapel like a sprig of lily of the valley. To the right, ahead of me, I noticed a pair of swing doors; when I opened these and passed through a small, interlinking antechamber bounded by yet more swing doors on the other side, I found myself inside the auditorium.

It was pitch-dark. I remained motionless for a moment to give my eyes a chance to block in the space. No usherette came forward out of the gloom to guide me to a seat, and the screen's as yet unfocused images – a beach, a tangle of semi-clothed bodies whose roseate flesh tints were as one with the sumptuously setting sun against which they were composed, an unexpectedly sudden shot of a crimson-and-yellow striped beach ball in gigantic close-up – confirmed that they must be fragments of a trailer or commercial.

As the contours of the auditorium slowly materialised, what struck me most forcibly was how sparse the attendance was: with those five or six rows nearest the screen completely unoccupied; with only an odd isolated figure, his knees propped nonchalantly against the place in front, in the half-dozen rows after that; and with the great majority of the public concentrated in one section on the left side of the stalls at the back, whether because it was from there that one had the best view of the screen or because regular cinema patrons have a natural and, so to speak, tribal disposition to bunching themselves together, to letting themselves drift towards seating areas given a seal of approval by those of their brethren already installed. It being the case, however, that my own disposition, as man and artist, consumer and creator, was to fly in the face of all such clannish conditioning, to persist in singing a song of my own amid a crowd singing theirs, and even, were ever that crowd to be collectively converted to mine, to begin singing a different song altogether, I strode down the aisle and took a place not only as far to the right as the 'public' was to the left but perhaps further forward than I would have been tempted to choose had everything else been equal. Having briefly sat down as though to claim the seat, I at once rose to my feet again and slipped off my scarf and overcoat. Then I sat down a second time and squinted quizzically up at the screen.

But I very soon started to feel oddly restless and ill at ease. On the screen, in the time it had taken me to settle into my seat, night had fallen. A cortège of young, garishly caparisoned and helmetless motorcyclists, hair flaming about their heads in the current generated by their machines, suddenly blasted out of nowhere; upon their manoeuvring a deserted street corner, the rear wheel of each and every motorcycle proceeded to skid in unnervingly vivid close-up until it felt as though its rider were about to be propelled right into the camera; and in the middle distance, presumably because of just this ungodly grate and screech of tyres, a row of windows began lighting up one after the other to mildly humorous effect. Whereupon, to my increasing perplexity, the scene shifted yet again. The spectator was invited to contemplate the somewhat implausibly ivied wall of a college; the camera at first closing in on two brightly illuminated windows in which could be seen, flouncing back and forth or flopping on to an enormous bed whose pink satin bedspread was heaped high with an unusually varied assortment of dolls, teddy bears and soft toys, a trio of giggling and chattering young women in different layers of undress and in one instance almost total nudity; then drawing back to reveal, beneath the windows, flitting about in a little thicket of shrubs and spying on the girls through a hotly disputed pair of binoculars, the motorcyclists of the earlier scene. I stirred more uneasily than ever. Already I knew in spite of myself that the motorcyclists' ringleader was called Cory or Corey and that, having somehow forfeited the affection of one Dora Mae, this Cory or Corey planned, as he informed an acolyte, a frightful-looking youth who went under the name of Kiddo and had acne, greasy slicked-down side-whiskers and a truly unprepossessing set of buck teeth, to photograph her in the nude and so blackmail her into continuing to 'date' him. Or something like that. But before I succeeded in mulling over that puzzler, one of the scantily clad young women happened to glance out of the window, saw the clandestine prowlers in the shrubbery and at once assumed a pose conventionally expressive of outraged chastity. There followed a fanfare

of girlish shrieks, the hasty drawing down of blinds and
the apparition in the college grounds of a battleaxe of a
headmistress-cum-matron sporting a grotesquely out-
moded pair of pince-nez on her thin, hollow-chambered
nose. 'Oh shit!' muttered Cory or Corey, and the whole
gang of voyeurs made a bolt for their motorcycles.

There was no doubt of it: this was the main programme of the evening. For some reason that eluded me
I was watching the wrong film. Scene followed scene,
one supposedly piquant incident succeeding another at a
bewildering rate. Seated far in advance of the body of
the audience, I was forced to turn my head to ascertain
whether anyone else but myself was disturbed by the
anomaly. Ostensibly not. There seemed to be no pro-
nounced enthusiasm for the off-colour antics on the
screen, but the very crassest and smuttiest of the film's
jokes had prompted a few uncouth guffaws, and certainly
no hint was audible of the anxious whisper of concern
that I would have expected to hear had everyone else felt
as I did. Yet such apparent indifference to what was
being projected in front of them, as though one film
were quite as good as another, was not what troubled me
most about my fellow spectators. It's true, I knew
nothing at all of the demographics of cinema audiences.
But these young people (for, excepting a dishevelled
tramp sitting alone, with four or five shapeless carrier
bags at his feet, in a seat on the left flank of the
auditorium corresponding almost exactly to mine on the
right, I was, and by far, the oldest person present), these
be-jerkined and be-jeaned young people, dangling their
legs across the seats in front of them and lighting up
cigarettes in insolently unsurreptitious defiance of an

illuminated 'No Smoking' sign on either side of the screen, scarcely tallied with my conception of the kind of public that might be attracted to a film version of a novel by Forster, no matter that it was one I myself had always regarded as something of a potboiler.

I turned forward to face the screen once more. The motorcyclists were on the move again, vaulting over a ridge in the roadway with such violence and abandon, one upon the other, that they seemed to take off into the air and momentarily hover there – an illusion, I suspect, having not a little to do with the low-angle frontality of the filming and perhaps the choice of a deforming camera lens. Fidgeting in my seat, I could not resist turning round yet again, and quite pointlessly so as I was aware, to study the public's reaction. Nothing. Plainly, it was the wrong film for me alone; and the rather complacent sense of self-reconciliation that I had enjoyed when entering the cinema had been dissipated once and for all as far as that particular Sunday afternoon was concerned. It was with sheer, undiluted loathing that I now considered the screen and the scrubby glamour of the Californian landscapes that appeared so stupidly at home there and the motorcycles parked outside a dilapidated café – this was a film that lost no time in advancing its narrative – and the hateful cyclists themselves who had squeezed together into a single booth inside and were drinking Coca-Colas to deafening juke-box music.

Enough was enough. I could no longer remain in my seat. An error had been made (not, I felt sure, by me), it would now have to be rectified. Although I scarcely relished the prospect, and recoiled from all such scenes, I would naturally have to ask the plump Filipina to reimburse me for my ticket. I quickly collected my overcoat and scarf from off the back of the seat next to my own and nervously felt inside the overcoat pocket into which I recalled having slipped my half of that ticket. And I was about to leave, was poised for flight, was actually starting to rise to my feet, when, in a manner that was almost pre-cognitive, that as it were allowed the essence of the sensation itself to precede by some while my understanding of the purchase it was to have upon me, something, something visible on the screen, arrested initially my gaze then my movement.

It has first to be said, though, that in the short period of my departure-taking a new departure had also been taken by the film's plot. Cory and his loutish minions had begun to eavesdrop on a whispered tête-à-tête conversation in the booth adjacent to their own; and, as though taking its cue from them, the camera immediately angled upwards, above Cory's eyes, his forehead and his lank and gummy black hair, above the panelled partition which separated the two booths, until it ended by disclosing, but only from behind, a cascade of shiny, synthetic auburn curls bow-knotted with a polka-dot ribbon. For the moment not much more than these curls could be seen, the curls and a downy, slightly elongated neck and a pair of shoulders and, glimpsed over the right shoulder, two hands resting upon a formica table top and clasped in two other hands, these being patently male if somewhat delicate and even childlike, and a glass salt-shaker and a ketchup container in the form of an oversized plastic tomato. Although neither face had yet been revealed, there could be no possible ambiguity: it was Dora Mae and her new boyfriend (even I, fussing over my leavetaking, managed to get the drift of the scene). At which point Cory, eager to learn who might be this unidentified 'dickhead' (his own esoteric epithet) with the tanned and slender fingers and faintly adenoidal voice who was paying suit to his own former sweetheart, stealthily edged up along the partition wall and peered over the top into the next booth; simultaneously, and seeming to match stealth with stealth, the camera made a slow and sinuous lateral movement to the left, a movement that came to rest only when, in virtual symmetry, it had framed the two faces, Dora Mae's and that of her suitor.

It was the latter face which had arrested my attention. It belonged to an adolescent of, as I supposed, about fifteen or sixteen, with fairly close-cropped blond hair, blue eyes with luxuriantly long lashes, a straight nose neither especially narrow nor especially pudgy and – for the moment the only ones perceptible in the sweetly reticent smile he offered up to the spectator's gaze – two ideally white but slightly crooked front teeth.

I could not help being astonished by the perfect beauty of the lad's facial features; and if I needed more time to register them fully, it was less because of my own fretful state of mind than because the textures of that beauty were both banal and extreme.

Banal, in that, despite an uncustomary gentleness of mien, the morphological type was one very much in the public domain; it exemplified what I take to be a specifically American criterion of 'cuteness' – which is to say, beauty untranscended by mystery, tragedy or spirituality, beauty golden and well nourished and so vacuously secure in its own natural and social prerogatives that, as much as heredity and environment, it is its very disregard or ignorance of other, less privileged species of late twentieth-century adolescence that appears to guarantee the tranquil perfection of sparkling eyes, of healthy white teeth, of a complexion tanned just so. But also extreme, in that I had never before seen so consummate a specimen of the type, one wherein all the knots of the face, so to speak, had been becomingly tied together, neither too tight nor yet too lax, one wherein each individual feature, so perfect in itself (with those rabbity front teeth constituting the single tiny flaw that is indispensable to perfection), had combined to form an incomparably lovely face-object. It was empty, depthless, pure surface; it was decorative, even rather enchanting, nothing more; but to have filled its void with meaning, with character, would have been in the cruellest and subtlest fashion imaginable to destroy it. There, I thought, is a face that will break a few hearts.

Still half-sitting, half-upright, my coat and scarf over my arm, I let myself sink back into the seat and now with head cocked in bemusement looked up at the youth. I had not changed my mind. I would leave presently. But having found myself once more in the mental posture with which I was perversely most at ease – that of being alone in apprehending the mark of beauty where it is least to be expected – I was determined to savour for a moment this unsummoned windfall.

That moment, however, was all too brief. Cory wasted no time in settling accounts with his 'baby-faced wimp' of a rival (as he contemptuously referred to him, with a venom that obscurely thrilled me). Almost at once a squabble broke out, one in which by virtue of his frailness of build the younger of the two was defeated with predictably ignominious speed. Emboldened by the subhuman cackle of his henchmen – and also, I was mystified to observe, by a smile of smug gratification from Dora Mae – Cory grabbed the boy by the fur-trimmed collar of his denim jacket, hoisted him bodily out of his seat and, displaying the wanton energy of a born bruiser, pitched him across the floor of the café. Heedless to his girlfriend's belated and in any case quite formulary protestations, he cast his eyes about for an instrument by which to deal out a final blow. They settled on the obscene tomato. With a half-witted grin on his face he picked it up off the table, stood astride the still supine figure and squirted the ketchup over him, from the roots of his hair to the tips of his white tennis shoes.

Having been played for laughter, the scene accordingly provoked a smattering of gormless haw-haws from the audience. And the sight of the victim lying on the floor, humiliated, fighting back tears, smeared all over with the foul red slop, while his tormentor slipped his arm around Dora Mae's shoulders and she gazed up at him with a beatifically coquettish smirk, of a sort that is intended to convey 'My hero!', was a uniquely grotesque one. Yet, to my eyes, tenderised by beauty, the ketchup bore an uncanny resemblance to blood, the actor to the dead Chatterton in Wallis's portrait. Forced to assume such a ridiculous pose, he somehow contrived to preserve the essence of all his coltish young charm.

I hung on a little while longer, reluctant to depart but just as reluctant to stay where I was. I couldn't let myself be exposed for too long to what was, save for the unsolicited *trouvaille* of a briefly glimpsed face, a film entirely without interest or distinction, an unqualified idiocy even for so disreputable an 'art form' as the cinema. And when it became plain to me that the actor in question was not immediately about to make a reappearance and that the film's protagonists were Cory and Dora Mae, I got to my feet again, took my belongings and, aware that a faint hot flush was rising in my cheeks, strode up the aisle and out of the auditorium.

Once in the foyer, which was now as deserted as when I had entered it, my insistence on being reimbursed seemed rather less pressing than it had been. Not only was I shy of confronting the placid little Filipina, who was still sitting at her glass-fronted cashier's desk, plump and olive-skinned, like one of those fairground automata that require a coin to be inserted if they are to whir into motion, but, as I told myself, the world for once had met me halfway, had come to me and made to my senses a small gift of beauty – beauty to whose existence I would not otherwise have been privy.

On the other hand I was as anxious as ever to satisfy my curiosity as to how and by whom the error had been made. On my way out I stopped again before the column of photographs which I had studied while sheltering from the rain. There they were, just as I remembered them, and there was even, atop the glass panel in which they were enclosed, the printed message 'This Week'. I confess I was utterly flummoxed, and on the point after all of re-entering the foyer and making my complaint to the cashier, when I thought to step around the column and take a look at what there might be on its other side. There, in an exactly similar display cabinet, were my old friends Cory, Kiddo, Dora Mae; there, in only one of the photographs, was my own particular discovery, in a setting which, as I noted at once, with a vague sentiment of regret, was wholly unfamiliar to me and which I therefore had to conclude belonged to that part of the film that I had not waited to see; there, too, inscribed on each of the stills, was the title of the film I had just walked out of. I could hardly bear to read it: *Hotpants College II*.

The cinema had two auditoriums, two screens, two programmes. The solution to the puzzle was simple, elegant and obvious. If it had succeeded in frustrating me it was merely that in my own day theatres had contented themselves with one stage and cinemas with one screen.

The rain had stopped. Opposite the cinema, above the dripping slate rooftops of the houses facing me from the far side of the street, there rose the slanting roof and gently thrusting steeple of a church, a church that I imagined as nestling in a glen of soft, wet, very English greenery, a roof and steeple shrouded in a fine, gauzy, silver-grey mist, as though painted by a Monet in dark glasses. I found myself smiling at that Monet image, one much too gaudy, too kitschy, ever to gain inclusion in my fastidiously unmetaphorical prose but also one, as I knew, more representative of my private, intimate, non-literary sensibility than many an admired passage from one of my books. Or it could have been at something else that I smiled. At any rate, smile I did. Then, turning up the collar of my overcoat, tying a robust knot in my scarf and tucking the two loose ends under my coat lapels, for the evenings were proving unexpectedly chilly for the season, I began to retrace my steps up Fitzjohn's Avenue towards Hampstead.

The next several days saw a perceptible change in my cast of mind. From being tetchy and self-absorbed I grew rather lighter, gayer, in spirit. For a day or two I continued to be affected by the whole bungled affair of the magazine interview. I could not hear the telephone ring (which anyway it did only infrequently) without imagining it to be the egregious features editor coming at last to apologise. But from that quarter there came no apology, no vestige of life whatever. It was almost as though, initially with the missed appointment, now with the absence of the merest sign of contrition, the magazine, its editor and one of its journalists had been engulfed in a vast and fathomless pit, never to be heard from again. Instead of discouraging me further, stoking up my animosity, such strange conduct actually had the effect of appeasing me, as might the antidote to a poison. I bothered myself once to ring up my agent, but he, it transpired, knew no more than I did.

Of very much greater significance was the fact that, on my return from the cinema, I felt stealing over me, quite spine-tinglingly, the idea for a new book, a novel. Idea, perhaps, is an overly grand word for what was just, at that stage, a miasma of intuitions and inspirations, a confused maze of thought processes. Yet I had begotten my four early novels in just that tentative and *décousu* fashion. The actual writing of them had been a relatively painless business and my post-composition labours a question above all of 'removing the stitches' from a prose style that was still to my eyes here and there disfiguringly scarred. It was the period of gestation that I found so painful. The line and form of what was to become my narrative had first to be carved out of a great unhewn slab of language. They were, I knew, buried in there somewhere, and it was the most supremely intoxicating joy I had ever experienced to sense them arduously emerge. Yet there were, as well, lengthy periods when impotence or just sheer incompetence would make me give way to despair, when I would simply panic and tremblingly cup my hands over my face and try literally to pull my hair out and deem myself worthy of being aligned with the most rank of rank amateurs. If these fits of enervation, as I paradoxically thought of them, were by now all too familiar to me, they did not terrify me the less.

With this brand new project, however, I was still the sculptor at that point in the process before the block of marble has been ordered, when it is the idea, not the accursed work, that is 'in progress', when it is the contours of the idea that have to be shaped and moulded and refined. Walking back along Fitzjohn's Avenue, passing the palm tree at no. 43A without even noticing it, I had had that idea – rather, two ideas. I would write a novel in the first person singular; and (this, I conjectured, was probably a first in English literature) its protagonist would be stone deaf.

The latter trope in no way represented a desire on my part to humanise my fiction with a crude injection of the pathos of disablement. I had as a writer a positive horror of what I would scornfully refer to as 'the tyranny of the subject'; my novels had never been, in any easily determinable manner, 'about' anything; and the new one, to which I cautiously gave the elegant, tragic title of *Adagio*, would assuredly not be 'about' deafness. What stimulated me in the conceit of a deaf protagonist was the strictly formal challenge that it would pose, the formidable puzzle of having to organise and articulate a narrative whose central character, whose conscience in short, would be incapable, on a pedantically literal level, of communicating with his fellows. That this disability could also be assimilated without too much strain into my personal thematics of sacrifice, and would therefore function for the more discerning of critics as what the French term an *effet de signature*, I was well aware. But I might claim in all simplicity and honesty that the idea had just 'popped into my head', as all my ideas did, and if it bore a strong resemblance to those which had preceded it, that could only be because it had sprung from the selfsame source.

I worked well and, despite those occasional seizings-up of despairing helplessness, reasonably quickly. I would rise early, at about seven o'clock. After a cup or two of sugary tea and a summary glance at my mail, I would settle myself behind the slightly tilted desk in my study. Thereafter, saving a short break for lunch, never more than half an hour, the only sounds made in that room were the stealthy ticking of the marble-framed clock on the mantelpiece and the soft scratch of my fountain pen – an amazingly slim, elongated silver model from Cartier, which had been presented to me one Christmas by my French publisher – as it filled the pages of my notepad. Invariably, at some time between four and five o'clock, I would start to tire or else feel reluctant to continue working by lamplight; without reading through what I had written, I would shut the notepad and slip it into the top drawer of my writing desk. It was then that, in virtually all weathers, I took my daily constitutional around the Heath, returning to the house an hour later to answer the mail and scan the newspaper and mix myself a dry Martini. I sat down to dinner promptly at half-past seven, and the evening hours would be spent either reading or listening to music – mostly German – on my Walkman, another Christmas gift, made from myself to myself, as I had a terror of disturbing my neighbours (which was in truth a terror of setting a precedent and thereby licensing them to disturb me).

Such was my daily routine. Conscious that the artist, no matter that his work may strike the world as the epitome of classical concision and grace, is himself a figure fatally cast in the Romantic mould, I wilfully courted the security and even monotony offered by such a routine as the indispensable counteractant to my more feverish bouts of creation. And I was, these few days, as contented a man as I was ever likely to be.

I even won a measure of personal satisfaction in the affair that had provoked me so. Now that I had regained my detachment, I thought the matter over and decided that I did not dare run the risk of letting it fester unresolved. I rang my agent again to enquire if negotiations with the magazine had already reached a contractual stage and, learning that nothing had as yet been signed, let him know that I was no longer willing to authorise the publication of extracts from my book and that he must resist any further overtures in that direction. Probably he was less astonished by this belated right-about face than by the initial acceptance – perhaps, too, he had reason to know that the editor would be relieved rather than otherwise to be freed from the burdensome obligation to which he had blindly committed himself. In any event, he received the instruction without comment and undertook to carry it out forthwith. The matter dealt with thus, the parenthesis closed, it almost felt to me as though the thing had never happened at all.

There was a single cloud on the horizon: my sleep was not of the best.

When in bed, on the far shore of consciousness, I had long possessed an eerie and inexplicable knack, that of conjuring up a gallery of faces whose features, if unrelated to those of anyone I knew, presented themselves to my inner eye in a hyper-realist wealth of detail: it was a knack which no longer disquieted me, even reassured me that sleep, real sleep, was about to envelop me.

These faces were disposed to a certain gaping-mouthed grotesquerie of character and expression, they were informed with an extraordinarily scrunched-up vitality and realism, their kinship (for in my waking hours I had given some thought to them) was with Daumier caricatures and Japanese masks and baroque, obscenely spouting gargoyles and caryatids. No sooner had they been evoked than they would generally start to fade, but many of them would leave a faint afterimage and next morning I would sometimes still remember the ones that had made the greatest impression on me.

For the last few days another type of face had begun to exhibit itself on the magic lantern of my semi-conscious mind, one whose features, blurry and spectral of outline, were not at first as piercingly transparent to me as the others. It was its very fuzziness which kept me from falling asleep, as I would struggle to bring it into sharper focus.

This happened four nights in succession. On the fifth, by virtue of so superlative an effort of concentration it seemed to me my brain might combust, I contrived at last to rip off the veil – which, uncannily, at the very last instant, fluttered away of its own accord, like one of those protective tissue covers in old-fashioned volumes of art reproductions – and the face that it had been concealing was disclosed. It belonged to the boy in the film.

I opened my eyes and picked up the alarm clock that sat on my bedside table. It was one minute to one. Although I seldom smoked in the bedroom, I usually kept, by the clock, a pack of cigarettes and a matchbox. Without switching on a lamp, I drew a cigarette from its open pack and lighted it. I inhaled deeply, then exhaled through my nostrils, tracing the whitish curl of smoke upwards to the ceiling. Halfway up, it was traversed by the shaft of light that filtered through from the street lamp just outside my front door and that had often chanced to remind me, appropriately enough, of the luminous cone that issues from a cinema projectionist's cabin.

The whole futile business had obviously nettled me more than I had realised, for this was the first time I could with certain knowledge attribute the paternity of a face from my night-gallery to one I had earlier glimpsed in daytime. Several days had passed since I had seen the film. Apart from stray lines of its dialogue which, imbecilic to the nth degree and occasionally bordering on the downright illiterate, had lodged in my brain against my will and of which, once in a while, I would find myself inopportunely reminded as I wrestled with my emerging narrative, I had put it out of my mind. I pondered the meaning of this little aberration, decided it had none; then, my cigarette only half smoked, stubbed it out in an ashtray and almost immediately fell asleep.

My work was also interrupted, if in more wonted fashion, by the arrival of a first complimentary copy of *The Gentrification of the Void*, followed a day or two later by nine others making up the full complement that was due to me. The latter would be sent to Cambridge graced with dedications that I seemed to have to agonise over as much as over the work itself.

It was, though, my practice to read the printed text through before sending out any copies at all – even if, having overseen each stage of creation and fabrication, I had become exhaustingly familiar with its every semicolon. I had to be the first to know what lay in store for the reader. I couldn't abide the thought of receiving a friend's flattering note of appreciation to which he then tacked on an afterword, doubtless sympathetic in intent but tending to the facetious in tone, about a line that was missing or a paragraph that had been printed upside-down. In this latest instance I did not discover too much to complain of, except for one 'literal' that caused me to die a little when my eyes rested upon it. To my horror, the name of Baudrillard, a 'thinker' I did not admire, had somehow been transmuted twice on the printed page into 'Bachelard' – a nonsense in the context. The error was all the more intolerable to me in that it was plainly not a misprint, that I could have ascribed to the negligence of a copyist or typesetter, but an unforgivably careless oversight on my own part. I scored through the offending name in each of the copies to be sent off to Cambridge and scribbled a laconic note in the margin beside it.

In the meantime work on *Adagio* was advancing well. It was firming up nicely, it was growing as hard and dense and compact between my hands as a snowball from which the fat, as it were, has been removed. The stimulus for having my protagonist speak in the first person had, of course, come from the revelation these few months back that I had never proceeded so in the past. That much was evident. But it was also my ambition to have him 'speak' in the literal sense and to contrast his stilted and faltering attempts to do so with the keenness and clarity of his mind as it would be revealed to the reader. Would I be able, I wondered, to simulate on paper the speech patterns of one born stone deaf – I who, as a writer, had never claimed onomatopoeic mimicry as being among my gifts? And would such an achievement, were it successfully carried off, not be bound to be regarded as tasteless and patronising in the extreme? One of my near-neighbours was a deaf-mute and she had been quite friendly with my wife. Although I had had little contact with her myself, and would see her hardly at all now that I had been widowed, I could still recall the curious moaning sounds that she had produced in her pathetic endeavours to communicate, speaking somewhat as one imagines one does oneself when under the influence of a dentist's anaesthetic. I made a few preliminary attempts on my notepad to reproduce these sounds in words, or sometimes just in letters strung along one after the other, and worked hard at it until I started to feel confident that I could carry it through an entire novel.

Absorbed in my labours, in these great and burning questions of art and representation, I erected a barrier between myself and the world outside; I was already something of an isolationist by natural inclination but the gestation of a novel would make me rigorously so. Once, some months before, around a dinner table, the conversation had turned to a young novelist in vogue and of universally acknowledged talent, who also possessed the good fortune to be the son of a novelist equally admired; and when I remarked to a question put to me that I had never read a line of his, my table companion jocularly turned to address me: 'What? Never read a line of X – ? *You've* led a sheltered life!' 'Only a fool would not wish or try to,' I coolly replied, aware that I was thereby reinforcing my personal 'legend', even among my closest acquaintances, as a self-willed solitary, practically a recluse.

It was not quite so – except, precisely, when I was at work; for then, struggling to forge my own language, I would refuse to let myself ever be distracted by what Mallarmé termed 'the words of the tribe'. I all but ceased to read newspapers lest my eye be drawn to, my brain obstinately register, some inept specimen of journalese, some insidiously punning headline that I would then worry at for days afterwards, since its very vulgarity would have made it next to impossible for me to forget. For the same reason I scarcely listened to the wireless any more, and read or reread only writers in a foreign language – even then, only those so far distant from my own sensibility in both period and world view as to render unthinkable the risk of any involuntary influence.

Yet, one afternoon, sitting at my desk, pen in hand, letting my mind wander as aimlessly as a schoolgirl's, I caught myself, to my surprise, thinking again of the youth from the film and wondering what could have happened to him after he had been sprayed with ketchup; wondering, too, what was taking place in the photograph that I had studied outside the cinema and whose setting had been unfamiliar to me – a garage, was the vague impression I had, what Americans call a filling station, or possibly some type of factory, for I seemed to remember a hint of piping in the background. At any rate, I idly told myself, it meant that he had not disappeared from the narrative, as I had assumed, after the incident in the café, that he must later have reappeared, probably more than once, and perhaps exacted vengeance on the awful Cory.

The thought passed dreamily through my brain that the boy might serve, in part at least, as a model for my protagonist (it was while seeking to clarify my thoughts on the character's age and physical formation that I had let myself slip into a state of museful reverie) and I tested out on him the same smooth, unlined brow, the same feathery blond hair and, above all, the same smile – a victim's smile. But even though, in order to facilitate the reader's identification with him (or rather, as I did not believe in such 'identification', his desire to *accompany* him through the meanders of my fiction), I meant my hero to be young, personable and bursting with health, unimpaired in every respect save that of his single disability, I soon laughed the comparison away, so ludicrous did it suddenly strike me.

Thereafter, however, at odd, unexpected moments, evenings, for example, when I might be reading in bed, the actor's face would resurge and press itself on my attention; venturing not to linger over it, as I did, would merely render it the more vividly present. I didn't know what to make of it all. It irritated me; and yet it also amused me as an unprompted and unwarranted little adventure of the spirit. What I did not feel, strangely enough, was any very real unease that my interest in the youth might be erotic in nature. Such as I remembered him at least, he was a lovely, flowerlike nonentity. If, as I fancied, adolescent girls fainted away as he passed, that was explained by the immaturity of their emotional lives recognising its natural correlate in the immaturity of his physique. And, a classicist by both education and temperament, I knew nothing more shaming and tedious in the literature of my contemporaries and near-contemporaries than the maudlin neo-Hellenist cult of the ephebe, with middle-aged men like Wilde and Gide tastefully salivating over sleeping youths and making mawkish comparisons with asphodels and eglantines. Yet this particular face had piqued my curiosity, this face I had not recognised was nagging at me like one I had recognised but could not name. I wanted to stand back, hold myself up to the mirror of my own self-scrutiny and conceptualise (here I thought with a grimace of the features editor) – contextualise my feelings on the matter.

I remembered that, while at Cambridge, I had been asked by the editors of an undergraduate journal, of the 'aesthetic' sort still more or less fashionable when I was up, to submit to the Proust Questionnaire. To the question 'What is it that most depresses you in life?' I had replied, 'The unequal distribution of beauty.'

On one level, the reply had been derisively intended, a wilfully provocative rejoinder (quite without consequence, to be sure) to what I considered to be the fatuous sham of any left-leaning political engagement among my privileged contemporaries. On another, though, it was a reflection of the almost religious fervour with which I had once prostrated myself before the world's beauty, and it could not have been more passionate and sincere (a contrast, in this, with most of my replies).

Yet if so exacerbated a type of aestheticism (now to be recollected with a sardonic smile) tends to be conventionally interpreted as a symptom or sublimation of homosexuality, such was not at all my own case. I had not once, not even at the feverishly lubricious public school to which I had been dispatched as a petrified ten-year-old, had what might be thought of as a homosexual experience. I could not even recall from those terrible and inexpiable years having felt burdened by the guilt of frustrated prurience, although I was always perfectly well aware of the nature of the heated fumblings and scufflings I would hear after lights out, the tiptoeing to and fro from one bed to another, the obscene little cabaret held evening after evening in the communal lavatory. No doubt I was undersexed, but, alone and aloof, I had never been exposed to the famous 'phase'. I knew myself, even then, to be 'boringly heterosexual', as I had later described myself to a wistful suitor at Cambridge.

As for the concept of bisexuality, so very modish now, I refused to take its premise seriously. The 'bisexual', so far as I was concerned, was a libeller of the self and of its profoundest instincts; to say the least, a victim of the most unproductive kind of wishful thinking. For me, indeed, he bore a droll likeness to precisely that unhappy young man who had clumsily propositioned me at university and who, in a foredoomed attempt to endear himself to me, had rattled on, slightly desperately, about how he loved 'every kind of music, from classical to pop'. But when, invited back to his room for a few dry biscuits and a thimbleful of sherry, I had had a chance to inspect his record collection, what I discovered was row upon row of obscure Broadway musical comedies and, tucked away out of sight as though in positive embarrassment and shame, certainly never turned to in the anticipation of any sheer, uncomplicated pleasure that they might afford, a classical library numbering no more than three records: Vivaldi's *Four Seasons*, naturally; a pairing of Mozart horn concertos; some vapid piano pieces by Satie.

Sex is destiny, is written – an injunction, a commandment, a ukase, to which no resistance, with which no compromise, has ever been possible. I had no great fears on that account.

Yet, far from expelling it from my system, I continued to be assailed by my strange and bothersome distraction, assailed as by a memory – a trivial memory, in truth, chafingly inconsequential, but lodged as naggingly in my mind as in the crevice of a tooth. By very definition, said Chesterton, our memories are of what we have forgotten. Perhaps, I said to myself one evening while taking a turn around the Heath, an excursion that would unfailingly calm jangled nerves and alleviate the burden of solitude, since I was all too ready to be deluded into believing that the loneliness I felt there, and especially at night, was a condition of the Heath, not of myself – perhaps if I no longer needed to remember, did not increasingly have to struggle to remember, the young actor's face, it would cease to be a memory, it would become as familiar to me as – and then I discovered to my astonishment that, my few Cambridge acquaintances aside, I could not think of a single other face in the world, or in that part of the world which constituted my world, that was not also merely a memory now, ever more fallible and dim.

It was on that day that I made my decision. As with a nettle I would firmly and ruthlessly grasp the flower. I would go watch the film once more (even in my inner-most thoughts, even mutely, I would not enunciate its title) and exorcise this odd little demon of mine. It was absurd, it was demeaning, but it had to be done.

When back home, and even before removing my overcoat and scarf, I went to my study. There I unscrewed the cap of my silver fountain pen and in the margin of the top page of my manuscript of notes, annotations and cross-references wrote a few scrawled words relating this new development in my own life, possibly with the intention of appropriating it for my book. But after a moment of introspection, judging that the contrivance, as I saw it, simply would not do for my protagonist (it was less his deafness than the idea that he would address the reader in the first person that troubled me), I drew a neat line through the marginalia, rescrewed on the cap of my pen, laid it down on the blotting pad at an angle exactly parallel to the pad on the desk and to the desk in the room and, ideally, to the room in the world, then left my study again, undressed and went to bed.

Next day I returned to the cinema at the foot of Fitzjohn's Avenue. As on that first Sunday, it was the latter half of the afternoon, but uppermost in my mind was neither the time of day nor the cinema's own timetable. It scarcely mattered to me whether my ticket would be purchased just as the film was due to start or else as it was already unfolding. All I wished was for the puzzle to be solved, seen to, done with.

What I had not calculated on, and learned only when standing beneath the overhang of the cinema's marquee, was that the film itself was no longer playing there. (Ironically, the photos of the Forster adaptation were still on display inside their oblong glass cabinet, but this time I barely glanced at them.)

I was nonplussed, made conscious as so often in the past, in very different situations, that the exhaustive precautionism of my working mannerisms had somehow never succeeded in influencing the fecklessness with which I engaged with the outside world. Just for example, it had taken me years after my wife's death, quite literally years, to assimilate the humble axiom that, to toast a slice of bread for myself alone of a morning, it made better sense to use the oven's single instead of double grill; years, too, to locate a shortcut from home on to the Heath that was very much quieter and more leafily rustic than the macadamised and car-infested route I had long been accustomed to frequent. And now I had, in the manner of the High Court judge who had asked 'What, pray, is a Beatle?' and to whom a hostile critic had many years before compared me, failed to realise that, *obviously*, in the way of such things, the cinema would meanwhile have changed its programme.

Was I then to turn back? To forget the rather foolish and humiliating purpose to my jaunt? That, I knew, I had come too far to do. And it suddenly occurred to me that there existed precisely a magazine whose function it was to help its readers locate a particular play, film or concert. My essay on angelism had been reviewed in it and I had been forwarded the piece by the cuttings agency to which my publisher subscribed. As I recall, it had been a very unfavourable review, vituperatively so, its author compounding his incapacity to follow the book's argument by an outstandingly insulting conceit: the culminating sentence, a direct quote from my text, was left half-completed and allowed to trail off in suspension points and a row of unequivocal little '*z*'s. Remembering how old and ridiculous and terrifyingly unfluent that review had made me feel, hardly daring to speculate on what course I might have embarked upon, I crossed the street to a small newsagent's shop and bought my very first copy of *Time Out*.

To begin with, I proved to be inadequate to this as to most other of those trifling challenges that the rest of the world seems to take in its stride. Standing in the open, hampered by a breeze tugging at the hem of my overcoat, protecting as I would a flame the fluttering pages of the magazine that were being flicked on faster than I could turn them, I was at once disconcerted by erratically captioned rubrics and headings and sub-headings and it was quite by chance that I hit upon a page on which the films of the week were listed alphabetically alongside the cinemas screening them. I let my finger slide down this list until it stopped on the film in question. Its title was punctuated by a colon, on the far side of which was the single word: Hammersmith.

I took my glasses off, from one ear at a time, as gingerly as a hiker on a country lane unravelling a strand of wool from the barbed-wire fencing in which his pullover has become snarled, and with the tips of my thumb and forefinger gently started to massage a sore and reddened hollow on either side of my nose. The street was deserted, save in the distance for the just audible hum of an approaching car. Replacing my glasses as carefully as I had removed them, I calmly raised my eyes and saw, before I saw the vehicle itself, the bright orange glow, fierce in the fading daylight, of an unoccupied taxi. Without further vacillation, indeed without reflection of any sort at all, I flagged it down. When the cabdriver looked out at me enquiringly, I heard myself say – heard, rather, my voice say – 'Hammersmith. The Odeon cinema.'

The experience of viewing the film again was a most curious one, satisfying inside the cinema itself but far from conclusive as soon as I was back outside, standing on one of those anonymous streets where of late, as I was forced to acknowledge, 'wryly', I suppose the word has to be, I had been spending so unconscionably much of my time.

During the whole eccentric expedition, which was

how I affected to regard my little outing, I miscalculated only twice.

The first occasion was actually purchasing the ticket. I had alighted from my cab to discover that the Hammersmith Odeon had no fewer than four separate auditoriums, which seemed to confront the potential customer like a multiple-choice question in an examination paper. That fact in itself posing no problem for me now, I immediately ascertained to which of the four I myself was bound; and, assuming a lopsided stance of tolerant impatience and negligently tapping my gloves on the knuckles of one hand, I asked for a single ticket for no. 3. The cashier, however, a slim, youthful, efficient fellow to whom a trim and dapper moustache lent an air of effete manliness (if such an oxymoronic condition is imaginable), made me name the film after all, despite having been given exactly the information he required, and, flushing pinkly, I had to stammer out the terrible title.

The second occasion concerned my wish to learn the actor's name. As chance would have it, the film had less than a half-hour to run when I took my seat in the small, steeply raked and claustrophobic auditorium. But it was only after having endured an unbroken chain of trailers and commercials, as well as the cinema's curtains being opened and closed and reopened and then reclosed with such inane regularity that I started to wonder whether the manager of the establishment were gripped by a horror of unveiling the white screen in its, to be sure, not quite pristine nudity, as though for him it represented the cinema's linen, its undies, its *unmentionables*, it was only after all of that and after the film had begun again that I realised that what I should have done was study its final cast roster or whatever it's called and that I would have to sit through it once more to the very end.

On reflection, though, the trip more than repaid the trouble it had put me to. The film itself had certainly not improved with age, and my tolerance for Cory and his motorcyclist chums reached a new low ebb. But I learned my favourite's name, a nicer one, I concluded, than I had any reason to predict in the circumstances: Ronnie Bostock. Ronnie Bostock. 'Ronnie' I had scant enthusiasm for, although, goodness knows, it could have been much worse; but the sound of 'Bostock' had about it an agreeably brittle, altogether un-Californian hint of Boston and New England, of which I had heard good and bracing things considering.

Ronnie Bostock. Was I, I mused, the only person capable of responding to such uncommon physical comeliness? Was I alone in tracing beneath the conventional surface a timeless and universal ideal, an almost supernatural radiance of pure heart, of innocent spirit and of the sun-inflamed flesh which expressed and enveloped it? Whatever dour puritanical vigilance I would once have sought to exert upon my emotions I now readily relaxed; the darkness of the auditorium, licensing me to watch without being watched, see without being seen, made my bored and restless eyes more lawless and brazen; and it was in a blissful mood of rapt and meditative tenderness – tenderness, yes – that I gave myself up, as I had never dared before to do, to a fantasy of pure contemplation. This bronzed boy looked as though he must smell of freshly baked bread. When he moved it was with the virile light-footedness with which one might imagine a statue to move. Ought I to confess that his smile, only his smile in close-up, with those two protruding upper teeth leaving a faint serration along the ripe redness of the lower lip, fairly enraptured me? The way, too, as tennis players do, he would wipe off the perspiration from his brow with the side of his upper arm and the inside cup of his elbow was delightful to watch. Never, I felt, could there have been such a sublime fluke of nature, and I thought again of the unequal distribution of beauty.

Although the boy had a relatively minor role in the film, one pretty much on the periphery of its narrative (if that is the word for so ragbag a miscellany of gross and near-scatological vignettes of student mores on the campus of a preposterously implausible American college), he made appearances in two or three scenes following that to which my eye had first been alerted. But also, as it transpired, in a scene just preceding the entry of the motorcyclists and obscurely familiar to me as something I had had partial glimpses of while settling into my seat. It depicted some sort of impromptu beach party got up by a dozen or so young people of both genders, their half-clothed bodies lent a patina of late afternoon warmth by premonitions of nightfall, by the shivers and shimmers of a Californian sunset whose sickly yellowish light would turn nearly to purple in its shadow pools.

Ronnie Bostock was prominently featured in it. He shifted in and out of focus, sidling dreamily along the beach, knee-kicking a football in the air, performing hand-stands, shimmying with his slender, almost invisible hips to raucous music from a massive transistor

radio set which lay half-buried in the sand like a bucca-
neer's treasure chest. He would follow the margin of the
shoreline barefoot, the diminutive shoreline of his own
feet overrun by the foam of incoming breakers as it
seeped between his toes. His slim, tanned legs were left
uncovered above the knee by a pair of sawn-off, tight-
fitting denim jeans. Over his torso, which one guessed to
be smooth and firm, neither bony nor too muscular, he
had on a sleeveless white cotton singlet on which were
stencilled the words 'My parents went to N.Y. and all
they brought me back was this lousy teeshirt', a joke of
sorts which, if not much more ingenious than most of
those in the film, did contrive to tease a smile out of me.

Later it was that scene that I would turn over and over
in my mind, trying to analyse why it had had such an
impact upon me. In my tiny kitchen, whose single
window overlooked a narrow, patchy lawn that I made
sure was tended in my absence (mutedly as it would
penetrate the cosseted fastness of my study, the dull
whine of the gardener's mower had ended by proving
fatal to my concentration), I sat sipping coffee, now idly
daydreaming, now reflecting on the bizarre little situation I seemed to have got myself into, a situation that I
was singularly ill-equipped to deal with. And I remembered something that had happened to me a long time
before. As a writer, I have never pandered to the cult of
the metaphor. I pride myself, even so, that I possess a
flair for the detection of what might be called the
'potential metaphor' – which is to say, the metaphor in
embryo, that for which no referent as yet exists. I have,
for example, been frequently struck by the fact of
retailers continuing to stabilise the prices of their goods

just below the round figures towards which they are so patently straining: a tape-recorder at £39.95, a second-hand motor car at £4999. I find it hard to imagine a customer naïve enough to be duped by so elementary a form of manipulation. But it has struck me, too, that such an ineffectual yet no doubt universal practice ought usefully to function as the metaphor of some more consequential abuse of society, even if I have still to discover what that might be. And, sitting thus in the kitchen, I recalled how, when my first novel was being typeset – and this at a period when I was relatively young and wholly without reputation – there had been one section of the printed text on which a long diagonal crack had opened up, a track of white, produced by the fortuitous disposition of words, or rather of the spaces between the words, which zigzagged down the middle of the page and, once remarked, drew the eye inexorably towards it. Typesetters traditionally hate these cracks and insist that they be taken out, the simplest solution being to ask the usually compliant author to remove or add a word or two, most congenially an adjective or adverb. But, inexperienced as I was, I had stood my ground, would not have harmed a comma; so that the typesetters, to their annoyance as also to that of my publisher, who reckoned he was doing me a favour by publishing the book at all, were finally obliged to readjust the pagination. If it were known, however, it was with a faint pang of remorse that I felt the disappearance of that fissure in my text, that white interstice of meaning, that involuntary calligram of negativity, that tiny San Andreas Fault upon which, unbeknown to me (for it was, of course, quite invisible in the manuscript), my

narrative had been erected; and I felt too, most power-
fully, that therein lurked a metaphor still in quest of its
subject.

Perhaps, it now occurred to me, I had discovered a
subject for it at last, in these features which limned
themselves so imperiously in the interstices, in the
negative space, as it were, of my own psyche; and with
dawning self-realisation it also occurred to me that, like
the arrogant and insufferable young genius I had been, I
did not want to be cured, or not yet at least, and that I
would suffer the disappearance of this nearly impercep-
tible crack in my being with an ache of nostalgia and no
little regret.

The following morning I rose unaccustomedly late
after a dream-filled night. But although I went immediately to my study, and by ten o'clock had already sifted
through the leaves of notes for *Adagio* and made a series
of minor annotations in the margin, I remained moody
and abstract. Later, I was astonished to learn for how
long I had allowed this debilitating state of affairs to run
on; it was just after eleven when next I glanced down at
the top page of my manuscript to realise that absolutely
nothing had been contributed to it in over an hour. With
an affected sigh of resignation I let my fountain pen slide
along the blotting pad, opened one of the little desk
drawers and drew out a leather address book on which,
in the upper left-hand corner, my initials were embossed.
For a few minutes longer I sat there, address book in
hand, and turned its pages one by one, at a pace leisurely
enough for me to scan each of them thoroughly. From
time to time, too, I would take up my pen again and
score through some name or other.

Then, just as the marble-framed clock behind me began softly to chime the half-hour, I stopped flicking through the pages to look long and hard at one in particular. I put the address book down and stood up; frowning, I studied the dial of the clock. Then I sat down again, stared at the open address book, lifted the telephone receiver and dialled a number.

I had not for years had any communication with Rafferty, save once, fifteen months back, when I had received an invitation to a cocktail party fêting his appointment as arts editor of a newly and, as it then appeared, rather rashly launched Sunday newspaper, an invitation concerning which I had not even seen fit to convey my regrets. This Rafferty, at the time when our lives had intersected, just once, briefly and without sequel, when my four novels were being republished in a collected edition, had written a lengthy and extrava- gantly laudatory essay on them in the *Times Literary Supplement* that I had publicly judged 'not stupid', by the faintness of which praise I had had absolutely no intention to damn. In fact, uniquely in my relationship with my reviewers, I had dispatched a discreetly phrased note of appreciation which was reciprocated by a far wordier and more effusive reply; and we had had lunch together, an unsettling experience for both of us and an experiment neither had ever sought to repeat. But if until the present Monday morning, and without having harboured towards my erstwhile champion the slightest hostility, I had lost contact with him, I had also for no very explainable purpose taken note of his new office number.

I knew at once from Rafferty's fulsome tone of voice

that no resentment lingered at the odiously condescending style in which he had been treated, fear of which had weighed upon me rather more than would ordinarily have been the case. Even so, plainly under no illusion that a call from such a source had been prompted by anything other than a request for some personal favour on my part, it was he who made the first move by politely enquiring how he might be of service to me.

I thought of my absurd and exotic mission, the query I was about to put into words, and was instantly struck down with stage fright. My teeth seemed to have got in the way of my tongue, the tongue itself to have lain down on the job. I started to stammer, to correct myself in mid-sentence, to preface myself and preface the prefaces. What further caused me to panic was the fact that before every phrase that, as I hoped, would once and for all explain the matter there always appeared to be at least one other phrase that would have to take precedence, so that my speech soon became a proliferation of niggling, clustering subordinate clauses, each one of them crowned by the next, and that by still another, and so on, interminably.

I was (I finally got around to saying) researching a novel, yes, after all these years, a new work of fiction, and I wondered how, for in this area I was a complete ignoramus, how or rather where one could find out what else a young film actor – or, indeed, actress – had done.

'What else?' Rafferty said after a long pause. 'I'm afraid I don't follow.'

'What else – what films, what other films,' the words

tumbled out helter-skelter. 'I mean to say,' I continued, 'films other than that in which one might have seen him.'

'Is it a real actor we're talking about?'

Possibly it was that I suspected a cynically insinuating inference behind Rafferty's question or possibly merely that, even from experience as yet so partial and limited, I had already come to acquire a lover's cunning and guile; whichever, I contrived to parry the other's suggestion of personal entanglement as nimbly as an old hand at the game. Alive to the juvenile thrills of subterfuge, I patiently explained that the protagonist of my novel was a film actor and that I myself had no idea where I would be able to find such clues as I might need to this kind of actor's film bibliography, so to speak.

'His filmography, do you mean?'

I thought I could detect, along the unbearably hissing telephone line, if not a low laugh, then an audible smile.

Nevertheless, just a moment after, my interlocutor was giving me the information I needed as though it were the most normal request in the world, listing reference works, books and magazines, from which such facts could be routinely obtained. And, having scribbled their names in a notepad that sat, until now virtually unused, beside the telephone, I abruptly wound up the conversation without even attempting to make the parodically vague overture towards a future meeting that tends to be the classic coda of such encounters.

For now that I had embarked unblushing on this adventure, I was becoming impatient to see its next phase through. The time for gnomic and unfruitful ruminations, for any coy and faint-hearted sidling about the object of my desire, was past; the time to take action, to assert my liberty, had arrived. I got up at once from my desk, slipped on my overcoat and stepped into the street.

God, usually of the Realist School, does on occasion dabble in the abstract. The morning sky was dappled all over with tiny puffy cloudlets, clean and white and arrayed above my head in a disposition of such four-square regularity it might almost have been made by a waffle machine; yet there was also an undercurrent of closeness to the air, as stifling as a heavy scent, that made me perspire under my coat. I walked so briskly that in a matter of just five or six minutes I had arrived at the newsagent's shop I was seeking.

Once inside it, however, I was dismayed by what at first seemed to me the hopelessness of the expedition. Not that the newsagent did not stock film magazines. On the contrary, there were shelvesful of them, mostly of a populist, gossip-mongering variety but with two or three containing learned (to all appearances, learned) articles on Russian, Spanish and Japanese film-makers of whom, naturally, I had never heard. I pulled them, one after the other, down from their shelves, rifled through them more and more cursorily and replaced them any old how.

But fortune, as would often be the case, was on my side. For as I prepared to leave empty-handed, I noticed a little further off, in another section of the shelving altogether, where not much more than its spine was exposed, an American magazine (a miniature dollar sign was just visible in the top left-hand corner), on whose cover, or that fragment of it accessible to the eye, was a photograph, of no more than postage-stamp dimension, a photograph of Ronnie Bostock.

Stealthily, lest someone, who could only be a fellow browser, were to observe what I was about (very afraid I was of appearing ridiculous), I eased the magazine off the shelf. It was called *Teen Dream* and Ronnie Bostock's photograph was just one, and among the less prominently displayed, of several portrait photographs on its front cover. These, superimposed on a constellation of gaudily coloured stars, all of different sizes, all radiating out from the centre, were (so I surmised) of the popular young film actors of the day, actors with such names as Kirk and Shane and Ralph and Jordan and even, unless I had somehow misread the meaning, River. Under each of them, moreover, was a caption bristling with exclamation marks and no doubt intended to entice the casual reader into the magazine. 'Why Kirk Says "I'll Never Make An R-Rated Movie"!!!' and 'Ralph's Storybook Romance!!!' and 'Could You Be The Girl Jordan Will Fall For???' And, under Ronnie's photograph, to which my eyes immediately darted, '20 Facts Ya Didn't Know About Him!!'. As someone who did not know any facts at all about him as yet, I confess I felt a certain onset of excitement, galled as I was at the same time by the one already manifest fact that my own favourite had had to make do with only two instead of the regulation three exclamation marks.

I opened the magazine. Its first page was devoted to a Message from the Editor, evidently a regular monthly feature. 'Hi, there!' this began. 'Summer's ended (a-a-a-a-aw!) but the fall's here (yay!) and the time is right'n'ripe for some cozy fireside r'n'r – which means rest'n'relaxation or rock'n'roll, dependin' on your mood!! All your favorites have been in a great mood since we last got together – and I've been in touch – I mean *personal* touch – with each'n'every one!!! Well now, just for starters – ' My eyes glazed over. Were I to have to read one more word of such twaddle, I felt, I could not be accountable for my sanity. I turned the page. There, among the table of contents, was what I was looking for: 'Ronnie Bostock: 20 Facts We Bet You Didn't Know About Him. Page 36'; and there, as well, in a separate, boxed-in little column listing the magazine's gallery of pin-ups, alongside Kirk and Shane, Ralph, Jordan and River, his name appeared again.

I did not turn to page 36. Instead, I calmly closed the magazine, glanced along the rows and rows of publications, selected a motoring journal with an enormous red sports car, sleek and streamlined to a degree, practically thrusting its way off the cover, and in some embarrassment – an embarrassment no longer my own but that, not, I fancy, unskilfully assumed for the occasion, of a family man commissioned by his adolescent daughter to buy her reading matter of which he has more than once had cause to express the mildest and most affectionate form of disapproval – I handed my two purchases over to a disarmingly apathetic shop assistant and paid for them.

In the street I wound my copy of *Teen Dream* into so tight a cylinder that no passer-by could have identified it and disposed of the motoring journal by dropping it into a litter bin very handily located just opposite the newsagent's shop. Then, with a spring in my step, I hurried back up to my Hampstead home.

★

I stood in front of the looking-glass over the mantelpiece in my study. *Teen Dream* was lying, still unopened, unperused, on top of my thick sheaf of notes for *Adagio*. For a long, long time I stood thus, examining my reflection. Finally, my motionless features creased into a gentle, recalcitrant smile; the ice was broken; the reflection smiled back. 'If,' I said to myself, 'if I affect a certain style, if I strike a certain pose, it's because I find it almost impossible to look at myself in the glass, even for the purpose of baring my soul, without at the same time straightening the knot of my tie.' And then (but solely because it did happen to be crooked) I straightened the knot of my tie.

Flushed and fertile with expectation, the expectation of at last grafting an objective reality on to a being who had not, not until now, not until this very instant, been any less spectral than the scrunched-up gargoyles' faces that had haunted me in my sleep (and, oddly, haunted me no more), I turned to the magazine I had just bought. With a trembling hand I opened it at page 36. The first thing to catch my eye was the 'pin-up' on the page opposite. Ronnie (I was on a first-name footing with him now) was shown in profile, rather *à la* Karsh, except that he had turned his head unsmilingly towards the camera, his chin resting in a somewhat stilted manner on the knuckles of his left hand, the thumb tucked lightly underneath as though 'chucking' it. He wore an unexpectedly bespoke-tailorish sort of white shirt with narrow, vertical blue-grey stripes; it would appear to have been just unpacked from its box on the evidence of an immaculate crease that my eye followed along the upper arm to the elbow and on to the generous cuff

which, because of the overly stiff and starchy press, did
not embrace as it might have the boy's slender, hairless
wrist; and around the rakishly unbuttoned collar, its two
wide flaps even more rakishly upturned on the neck,
hung a loosely knotted grey woollen tie. There was
something about the shirt, the open collar and the
woollen tie that conjured up the conventional image of
the English public schoolboy. Something, too, about the
pose, half in profile as it was, as though the model were
bending over a chair, which made me think, hard as I
struggled to expel a thought so squalid, of just such a
schoolboy compelled by his fellows to receive a caning
on his bared buttocks.

His hair was longer, and seemed blonder, than in the
film. It tumbled in underneath the turn-up of his collar
at the nape of his neck with the odd, randomly
uncombed tuft poking out over the top. His eyebrows,
of a much darker shade than his hair, darker than by
rights they ought to have been in someone so fair, and
threaded by single strands of real auburn, softened the
high-toned purity of his unlined brow. His marbly blue
eyes might have been polished they shone so. Withal,
this face was not a flawless one. Since his lips, slightly
pursed, were closed, the teeth were concealed. But I
remarked a spot, a minute beauty-spot, no doubt, just
above the corner curl of his upper lip; and another, also
located on the right half of his face, nestling beneath the
nostril's soft shell. Otherwise his complexion was quite
perfect, captured by the photographer in all the poignant
bloom of adolescence and looking (so it struck me) to
having not yet suffered the coarsening attentions of a
razor blade. He was – a fact I would never have believed

possible – even more exquisite than on the cinema screen.

I started to read, word for word, from the first line to the last, the accompanying article. It was couched in the same noisy, ejaculatory idiom that the Editor's Message had been, but I had cast my scruples to the wind and I greedily devoured it. And how much I learned that was surprising to me. I learned, for example, that Ronnie had been born on the 8th of March, 1970, so that he was just twenty, at least three or four years older than I had once reckoned; born and brought up in the San Fernando Valley in Southern California. That 'his dad is Ronald, Sr, his mom is Lucille, kid sister Joanie and current pet a mixed-breed pooch named Strider'. That his favourite food was 'fast food – I call it fast food 'cos I have to fast after eating it!!' That he preferred girls who 'are sincere, romantic, have a sense of fun and who like me for *myself* – not just 'cause I'm a star'. That he found making movies 'neat' but hated 'all the razzmatazz – and specially all the waitin' around you have to do!!'. And that he would kiss a girl on their first date together 'only if she made it clear she wanted me to'. Besides his acting gifts, he was apparently 'an accomplished jazz drummer' whose greatest ambition was 'to play the drums in an upcoming movie – preferably opposite Madonna!!!' Had he ever been in love? 'Who hasn't?' Pet hate? 'Designer stubble.' And his secret, unspoken fantasy? 'To go to bat for the Mets.'

I sat at the same desk where only lately I had laboured over the genesis of *Adagio*, intently reading and re-reading each of the youth's answers, interrogating them for any, not immediately tangible, clue that they might offer to his more latent psychology, even as the mute and unshakeable conviction was growing within me that the whole piece, questions and answers alike, could be nothing else but an outright fabrication on the part of the editor, doubtless with the passive collusion of Ronnie himself or his agent.

Yet, no matter how questionable its provenance, this information was all I had to work upon for now and I feasted off every last crumb with a zest of appetite that few books had given me lately.

Most significant, though, was what I learned about the lad's professional life. It transpired that Ronnie had 'made his showbiz debut' advertising 'sneakers' on television commercials, had been cast in some 'popular, long-running sitcom', whatever that was, and had to date completed just three films, that which I had already seen and two others, tersely and enigmatically titled both of them: *Tex-Mex* and *Skid Marks*.

After a moment's hesitation, I rose from my desk and stepped into the perennially gloomy hallway and over to a small, oblong combined-table-and-umbrella-stand on which, the evening before, I had left my copy of *Time Out*. I quickly ran through its pages to the one on which were listed the films on current release. Neither of the two titles appeared on it; and, of course, I was not to know how long ago the films had been made or whether in fact they were still in circulation. For the moment, there was nothing for me to do but return to my study and continue perusing that inexpressibly foolish but precious text. And when I had finished, when I felt I had extracted from it all it had to give me, I unlocked a desk drawer and placed the copy of *Teen Dream* inside it, face downwards.

What differentiates a true obsessive from the mere addict, the alcoholic or the unrequited lover, whose monomania will eventually seep into every vacant pocket of his existence, until it comes not merely to coincide with that existence but actually to expand at such a rate, to such a monstrous dimension, that it ends by encompassing, overwhelming, it, making the existence just a part of the mania as once that mania had been just a part of the existence – what, I say, differentiates a *true* obsessive is that although, as was true of me now, he does not seek and would vigorously reject a remedy for his mania, he yet contrives to contain the hold it has upon him within an organically determined perimeter, where it may all the more deliciously suppurate. And this brings in its train a sense of exacerbated self-mastery, an almost intoxicating sensation of power over both the obsession itself and the outer world: the first because, so far contained, it must come to seem for ever containable; the second because the world will remain always unaware of its influence over him, so seamlessly decorous, so impenetrably respectable, even bourgeois, becomes the façade he erects between it and himself.

In the weeks that followed, my obsession with the young actor grew apace, demanding more and more of my time and my energies. Yet, by indulging it to the fullest, I was also alleviating it. My novel, now so radically transformed it bore only a titular relation to the original project, flowed as fluently from my pen as though the complete narrative had somehow been miniaturised in advance and injected into the nib and it were merely a matter of posing the pen over the paper, teasing each word, like a droplet of ink, off its tip and having it spill on to the blank page. Effortlessly, and at an earlier stage in the process than had ever been the case with me, I passed from annotation to composition, manoeuvred with ease, word upon word, sentence upon sentence, the labyrinth of my fiction. If it was writing itself, of all the successive stages attendant on the production of a novel, which had always been the least painful and laborious for me, I had never in the past known such a state of jubilation and grace.

I worked exclusively in the morning, however, my afternoons being reserved for Ronnie. Having learned, having all but memorised, those '20 Facts' about the actor, I wanted now to learn everything I could. And on making enquiries at the shop where I had bought *Teen Dream*, as to where I might find other American magazines – I was careful to leave their precise category discreetly unspecified – I was informed of a newsagent's in Soho that was, I was told, frequented by half the city's émigré population.

Off I sped, then, to this cosmopolitan emporium, where one actually *did* have the impression of all the world's languages being spoken – in print, at least. Thousands, literally thousands, of publications, ceiling-high and classified by nationality, were racked along three of the shop's four walls. And the American section, so comprehensive that it alone seemed to take up practically a whole wall, was further subdivided according to the specialised interest to which each type of magazine catered: *News*, *News Analysis*, *Sports*, *Fashion*, *People* and, usefully arrayed on adjacent racks, *Movies* and *Teens*.

For the cinema section alone it would scarcely have been worth leaving Hampstead. There was just one magazine (whose name, *Video*, the classicist that I was could not help for a split second reading as an elementary but in the context unexpectedly literate allusion to the Latin, before it dawned on me that it must refer to the current fad for videotape recorders) that contained anything at all about Ronnie Bostock: a small, ill-reproduced colour photograph from *Tex-Mex* in which, his hair dishevelled, his jeans grubby and torn, his face a livid mask of terror beneath a balefully luminous moon, he was being dragged feet first under a barbed-wire fence by a pair of Mexican-looking youths, both of them, as I noted, swarthily handsome brutes.

Already clutching that magazine, I started to flick through those under *Teens*. And, there, I simply could not credit my good luck! There were five of them, and they would have been in every respect indistinguishable one from the other had it not been for their names, all of them artless permutations on the words *teen*, *beat*, *dream* and *young*. Extraordinarily, not one of them was without its gushing tribute to the actor – rather, it seemed extraordinary to me, since I had not yet understood that, although Ronnie's career in films could still be considered no more than promising, and even then only just, the quality of his physical 'puppiness' had already made him an icon and idol of clammy prepubescent fantasising. The tributes, too, would prove to be virtually indistinguishable, except for the half-dozen monochrome and occasionally rather fuzzy snapshots that made up their illustrations. Here was Ronnie, boyishly resplendent in a snow-white junior-sized dinner jacket stepping out of a 'stretch' limousine for an evening on the town. There, curled up on a sofa in his 'den' and hugging adoringly to his breast a large and very hairy dog of, to my untutored eye, indefinite breed, presumably Strider. Here, in a stylish, loose-fitting track suit jogging along a high coastal road with, in the distance, dewily out of focus, a white steamship crossing a sound. And there, in quite the most endearing of all the photographs, taken against a featureless and flatly lit studio backdrop, Ronnie contracting his whole body into a curve and hurtling upwards in a flying leap, almost as though he were juggling his own limbs in the air, with such an immoderate release of pent-up energy that his teeshirt was starting to edge up over his belly and expose the belly-button – a pose, however painstakingly imagined in advance, however often rehearsed with the photographer, than which nothing could have struck one as more joyously spontaneous and life-loving.

At the colour pin-up portraits I cast only a perfunctory glance. Like a schoolboy who resists opening the latest issue of a favourite comic-book until such time as the stage has meticulously been set for it to procure him the most acute of pleasures, I was determined that only in the intimacy and tranquillity of my study would I bring to them the intense and detailed scrutiny they deserved. This time, though, as I realised, glancing furtively at the shop counter and the bearded Indian or Pakistani gentleman who was standing motionless behind it and following my movements with an expression of benign expectancy, as though he were anticipating a good sale, I could no longer, with five almost identical 'teen' magazines to be bought and paid for, plausibly cast myself in the role of indulgent parent to a teenage girl. Even knowing as I did that my motive in buying these magazines was of absolutely no interest to anyone save myself, some such role would nevertheless be required if I were to pay for them, be handed my change and depart from the shop without suffering any unduly protracted agony of embarrassment. So it was that I laid them down on the counter and opened my wallet – they turned out to be rather costlier than I had mentally bargained for, and I started slightly on seeing the sum that was rung up on the cash register – while assuming, in an ineffably subtle manner, the air of some social theorist, some professional analyst of mass culture, obliged by the very special nature of his research to buy in such otherwise preposterous bulk. And whether or not the Indian newsagent, for whose sole benefit the charade had been played out, was appreciative of the performance – his unfailingly, inscrutably dulcet monotone betrayed no trace whatsoever of irony – it had served its purpose as far as I myself was concerned.

These magazines rewarded thoughtful study. Not caring, however, to keep around the house what constituted for me so much dead matter – which is to say, everything in them that did not pertain to Ronnie – I spent the earlier part of the evening clipping out articles and photographs and pasting them into a cuttings album I had once purchased but never used. Then, much later than usual, I went on my daily stroll around the Heath. This once, thrillingly, the stroll would have an objective other than its statutory one of soothing my nerves. Instead of aimlessly circling that stretch of the Heath that remained more or less in sight of my own house, I headed directly for the part of it which was furthest from home, a wilder and more densely overrun area than I generally frequented, traversed by the long and purplish shadows of the enveloping dusk. Feeling after a while that I need walk no further, that I had at last cleared the magnetic field, so to speak, of my own house and those of my neighbours, I peered about in the gloom for a litter bin; found one which had been rigged up to the trunk of a solitary beech a few yards away and which was already overbrimming with assorted lager cans, potato crisp packets, used prophylactics and the wrapperless, picked-clean remains of someone's fried chicken; and, first making certain I was not observed, stuffed the magazines one by one into the disgusting mulch. Then, a shiver running through me, I strode back homewards.

Since Ronnie was just out of his teens, even if crucially older than I had assumed him to be (but ages, I had come to understand, had to be judged by criteria different from those in force in my own young days since 'age' itself seemed meanwhile to have been rejuvenated), the so-called 'biographical' material that the magazines traded in tended to be of a deliriously self-duplicating and self-perpetuating type. It was merely the rubric that changed. In the first it was '20 Facts We Bet You Didn't Know About Ronnie'; in another, 'Ronnie – The Hottest Rumors Whispered in Tinseltown'; in another, 'His Dreaminess, R.B.' (which had for me an incongruously

Firbankian ring to it); and if, in a fourth, the form adopted was that of a straightforward interview, just the sort of interview, indeed, that I myself had been willing to submit to only a few weeks before, its subject uncannily assumed the same exclamatory tone of voice as the (uniformly feminine) gossip-mongers when writing about him. Time and again (for this initial investment of mine was to be only the modest foundation stone for a collection of what I might term Bostockiana or even Ronniana that would be the envy of many an adolescent girl) I would read of Ronald Sr's prosperous real estate business; of Ronnie's own secretly entertained hope (a secret divulged in at least three of the magazines without any of them heeding the paradox of calling it so) that he might one day be cast in a movie as the son of his favourite actor, one Jack Nicholson; of his idea of the 'perfect date' ('a Mets game followed by a candlelit supper in an intimate and romantic French restaurant'); of his sentiments towards his 'legion' of fans ('tho I mean to graduate soon to more serious parts, I won't ever forget that they made me what I am today'); and of his attitude to R-rated movies ('Yes, I guess I'd do a nude scene, but only if it was tasteful and essential to the story. But I'd take a lotta persuading. I mean to have a whole litter of kids someday and I wouldn't want them to see their dad pawing some half-nude woman'). How often, too, did I read – with something of the doting complacency of a fond father for whom such stale trivia has become the source of inexhaustible, ever replenished pride – about Ronnie and marriage ('Will I ever marry? You better believe it!!!'), Ronnie and drugs ('Never touch 'em. Never have, never will'), Ronnie and smoking (he had lit up a cigarette just once in his life and it would never happen again 'except if a part called for it'), Ronnie and success (he believed it was every actor's duty to work for charitable causes 'to pay his dues to the world that had dealt him a winning hand') and Ronnie and the commercial failure of *Tex-Mex* ('I was devastated. This was one movie I really believed in and wanted to get its message across'). And I would repeatedly lavish loverlike glances on the photographs that illustrated these texts, as though endeavouring to verify beyond any shadow of doubt that such trite, repetitious and infinitely charming utterances could have passed the lips to which they were attributed.

Reading them, too, called to my mind a curious incident from that most unhappy period of my schooldays, one I had long since forgotten. Until the summer break in question most of my daily energies had been expended in warding off the ragging and bullying of which my timidity, fragility of build and quite unintentional priggishness of manner combined to make me a prime target. Nor had I helped the situation by being utterly hopeless at cricket, soccer and rugby alike, by consistently confusing the rules of the two latter games and, for all of nine years, failing to grasp even the rudiments of the former. During the fourth year of my attendance, however – my holiday at home having coincided with the last stages of my grandfather's lingering death – I had been delegated to read for two hours or so each day, throughout what turned out to be a cheerlessly waterlogged season, at the bedside of the ailing but still alert old gentleman. Although I read aloud all manner of literature, from Dickens to Dickson Carr, what my grandfather most enjoyed were *The Times*'s reports of that year's Test series. And if the rules of the game were ever to elude me, those daily sessions in the sick room, with its perpetually drawn blinds and its intriguing aroma of suspect cleanliness, ended nevertheless by making me exceptionally knowledgeable on the progress of that particular competition, on the strengths and weaknesses of both teams and the individual exploits of virtually every player. Enriched by this unearned little bonus of cricketing lore, I returned to school in the autumn and was soon enhaloed by an expertise that carried all the more prestige for being so inexplicable.

Now, I would think at odd moments of the day, laying my pen down on the blotting pad and gazing blankly out of the window, imagine the hubbub I would cause were I to drop in on my Cambridge acquaintances and recite to them everything I know of an obscure American actor of whom they would never have heard and to whose one feature of interest they would be totally insensitive. Only I, I exulted, only I and that legion of fans who do not count, have recognised this rare flowering among weeds, this unique compatibility of form and flesh, this *fait accompli* of physical perfection. But then, I went on, brought up short by another fancy, can it be that I am still the person I was, a respectable middle-aged widower possessed of a culture and erudition far in advance of the generality, and yet find myself appearing to share the sexual tastes and fantasies of an American teenybopper? And if I am to remain true to the implications of these tastes and fantasies, should I not now withdraw my cuttings album from the little coffin of a desk drawer inside which I keep it concealed, remove the pin-ups of

Ronnie and do with them precisely what the word itself tells me to do – pin them up? Pin them up on one of my bedroom walls? Perhaps I might even send off a stamped addressed envelope to the studio in Hollywood care of which Ronnie can be contacted by his fans and from which signed photographs are promptly sent back to them – there being no mention of any age-limit in the advertisement I cut out of *Dreamboat*, apparently no discriminatory objection to one of these fans being a not too young English writer based (as *Dreamboat* would put it) in Hampstead, England, and whose works are regarded, by his publisher at least, as Modern Classics. For I did cut the advertisement out – and why, for heaven's sake, if not to make use of it in the manner prescribed?

There was, I believe, nothing as yet in my external demeanor, in the course of my modest daily traffic with the world at large, by which the bitter-sweet compulsion to which I had surrendered might chance to be betrayed. Except on those occasions when I was obliged to dispose of the waste matter, the superfluous connective tissue, of those magazines of which I was now a regular consumer, and hence had to find my way to a litter bin far enough from my own home for them not to be traced back to their owner – and a feeling of delicacy, a qualm, something close to paranoia, deterred me from ever making use of the same bin twice – I would set out for my constitutional over the Heath at an identical hour more or less every afternoon. Once a fortnight, as I had done off and on for nearly eighteen years, I would visit a seedily opaline hammam in Jermyn Street for a massage and steam bath: there, lying out on a cold slab like the living sarcophagus of a warrior saint, my eyes half-closed, my arms crossed on my abdomen, my fingers interlaced, there, enveloped in white towelling and flanked by veiny green colonnading, I would let myself be pummelled by a pair of young fists with the words 'Love' and 'Hate' tattooed across their knuckles. My *Telegraph* flopped through the letter-box each morning along with the mail, my linen was sent to a local laundry twice a week to be collected three days later by my housekeeper – in or out of doors, if ever my movements risked being spied upon, I would let the world see me to be as absorbed as ever in the serene, thin-textured minutiae of my existence.

Yet with each day now came an intensification of my secret life. I was, for example, thoroughly briefed on everything pertaining to the magazines that brought me news of Ronnie. I knew in which half of the month they were published in the States, how much later after that were they available in the United Kingdom and in which of the two Soho newsagents' shops I frequented could they first and more easily be found. I would instantly, now inside the shop itself, scan their contents pages to note whether there was an article of interest and concern to me. Almost invariably there was such an article; but should it happen that I was not so favoured by circumstance, I also knew which of the magazines' more general features – 'Shhhhhhhhhhhhh!!! Don't Tell A Soul, But . . .', 'Flick-Flack', 'The Gossip Gazette' – might possibly contain a juicy item of information, some anxiety-inducing shred of 'tittle-tattle', on Ronnie's doings. Or else a photograph of him attending a rock concert in Madison Square Garden or playing Trivial Pursuit 'with a few of the guys' (but who were these 'guys', I would fitfully wonder, and what precisely did they mean to him?) or posing in a pair of gorgeously palm-patterned Bermuda shorts around the family pool with Mom, Dad, little sister Joanie and, inevitably, bringing up the rear, Strider the mixed-breed pooch. I had even conditioned myself by now to the intemperate spout and gush of prose, the indiscriminate ooze of enthusiasm, the scattershot spray of exclamation marks, that I would rationalise to myself as the very onomato-poeia of youth, energy and, why not, sex appeal. And I would browse and buy in either of the newsagents without now attending to, probably without really notic-ing, the quick, sly glances I began to receive, the quaint sidelong bemusement I had once so prematurely feared and thought to detect, the studied little finger flick, so negligently effected as to seem perfectly routine, with which the shop assistant would slip the magazines into a plain buff envelope before handing them to me, a doubtful compliment, I knew, but I no longer cared.

There was one point, however, on which I felt a very real frustration: I had still to see *Tex-Mex* and *Skid Marks*, those two previous films of Ronnie's about which I had read often and, so far at least as *Tex-Mex* was concerned, tantalisingly. It seemed to me scarcely prac-tical that, once released, a film should vanish into a limbo of neglect from which it could not subsequently be recalled. And self-knowledge had taught me that if ever I was struck by some such apparent malfunctioning in an area about which I was ill-informed, then the likeliest eventuality was that I lacked a crucial element by which all would explain itself. There was a way to see these films, I decided, and it was for me to discover it.

Thus I rang up Rafferty again, coming straight to the point with a question about catching up with older films – which was not to say, old films, or so-called 'classics', but films that were no longer going the round in London's cinemas. On this occasion I knew at once that my call had been ill-timed. Rafferty seemed busy, distracted – perhaps, though, he was no busier than during my first call but merely disinclined to lend his full attention to a disappointingly mundane enquiry, no matter that the enquirer was a man he admired. In any event, our conversation was interrupted more than once by an interpolated query from some underling in the newspaper office, a query to which (as I could not help remarking, with a vague sense that the esteem in which the other held me had already been eroded) Rafferty's own response sounded less brusque and impatient than it ought to have been had he considered the telephone call to be of the first importance. There was, too, the fact that even when we were left uninterrupted, I heard a faint tap-tap-tapping in the background, as though Rafferty had continued to labour away at his infernal computer while turning a merely half-attentive ear to the problem in hand.

It was in a voice of listless incredulity, as though even one so prone to cultivating an air of fogeyish unworldliness as I was really ought to have heard of the phenomenon, that he told me of the popularity of video recorders and tapes, as also of the high-street stores from which such 'hardware' and 'software' were to be bought or rented.

I took note of this information in a hand that was neat, methodical and businesslike. Although I grew conscious, as I posed more and more questions, that if I were indeed supposed to be researching a new novel the dry, incorruptible austerity which in the past had always been the glory of my fictional style would hardly be equipped to accommodate such a profusion of naturalistic detail, there had come into my dealings with the world, involving Ronnie, such a blithe and reckless irresponsibility, such a mad and total disregard for subterfuge or simply for the conventional attributes of discretion, that I ended the call by thanking Rafferty for his kind assistance without, this time, attempting to justify my need for so many factual particulars. I even went so far as to propose that he and I 'have lunch together some day', albeit with that airy indefiniteness of tone that tends to mean not 'some day' but 'some sunny day', which is to say, never.

And just two days later I became the owner of not only a video recorder but a television set, my first as it happened. In fact, I had failed to grasp from Rafferty's explanation that any use of the former was contingent upon prior possession of the latter, and I had had the mortifying experience of ordering a splendid new and jet-black recorder, its panel of controls such as I imagined could not be equalled but by the dashboard of a supersonic 'plane, and having it delivered to my home only to find the delivery boy snickering at me in disbelief because I didn't have a television set.

Eventually this too was put right, the two umbilically

linked machines were installed inside my study, on bookshelves which had to be hurriedly cleared of a complete collection of Balzac. Holding the manual in one hand, I experimented with the sample tape I had received with the recorder. Then, confident that I was as proficient at the controls as I was ever likely to become, I immediately made my way down through Hampstead Village to its sole video-rental shop, whose address had been given me by the same snickering delivery boy and in which I had not the least difficulty finding, with my greedy, picky fingers, tapes of both *Tex-Mex* and *Skid Marks*.

It wouldn't be easy to describe the excitement with which I advised my housekeeper (rather redundantly, in truth) that I did not wish to be disturbed, locked the door of my study, settled myself as comfortably as I could on a cushion that I placed on the floor (for some reason connected with plugs and sockets, the recorder and television set had been positioned on the lowest shelf of my bookcase), inserted the tape of *Tex-Mex* into the dim, dark letter-box slot, nervously prodded the appropriate button on my remote-control unit and rested my head back on the conch-whorled fist of a narrow Empire chaise-longue that stood, like a psychoanalyst's couch, close to the curtained window.

To start with, though, I forgot to switch the television set on at all; then forgot that there was, of its twelve channels, one alone designated to receive a video image and only remembered when the television programme, a witless show about sheepdog trials which surely no one could have wanted to see, ran on imperturbably, quite unaffected by the fact that the recorder was already humming away nicely; and then forgot which of those twelve channels was the one so designated and had to proceed by trial and error from channel to channel (it turned out, as might have been predicted, to be the twelfth and last of all). Yet these mishaps only sharpened my appetite for what was to come after.

Of the two films, *Skid Marks* was the more negligible, and not merely because Ronnie's own part in it was negligible, hardly more than that of a walk-on. To my dismay, its narrative revolved yet again around a gang of motorcyclists, based in this instance in San Francisco. Of two rival gangs, I should say, whose anti-social escapades – forcing motor cars off the road, crashing headlong into a plate-glass window, causing a terraceful of diners in some harbour-side restaurant to scatter for the sake of life and limb, smashing to smithereens a huge oblong tank filled with live fish which made up one entire wall of the same restaurant, swan-diving off the end of a nearby pier straight on to the upper deck of a white and streamlined yacht moored in the marina – were portrayed in the film as though nothing were likely to impress the spectator as more delightfully larky and irrepressible.

Thankfully, Ronnie had only a small part to play in these reprehensible antics. He was cast, rather against type, as 'Prof', the younger brother of one of the motorcyclists and, one gathered, something of a high-school swot. As a precocious scientific wizard and inventor (notably of a rickety retroactive rocket which was attached to his brother's cycle with the expected crude comic effect), he had been burdened with a pair of owlish spectacles that would repeatedly slide down the bridge of his nose, a mop of hair that I rather longed to run my fingers through and a droll and otherwordly air of beetle-browed quixotry. Oddly enough, it was he to whom had been assigned the line of dialogue from which the film's title was punningly derived, a line whose stupendous vulgarity took my breath away even as it did make me laugh. It was delivered by the actor in the scene directly succeeding that which I mention above, when, after a series of violent twitchings and backfirings, his hand-crafted rocket device had caused the cycle to which it was attached to jerk itself into the air, forward and upward at the same time, completely out of the control of its rider, who then landed, rear end up, in an enormous compost heap. Dragging himself from the mire, he discharged a volley of obscenities at the unwit-ting agent of his disgrace, who, alarmed at first, was now helplessly doubled up with laughter. And it was at that moment that Ronnie, drawing himself up to his full height and making an indecent gesture with the fore-finger of his right hand, spat back at his brother with all the adolescent aplomb of which he was capable, 'And you . . . you know what you are? You're nothin' but a skid mark on the underpants of life!'

Never in my life had I encountered this figurative use of the phrase 'skid mark', but the image was so shock-ingly vivid, so instantly, hideously legible, that I threw my head back and let out a laugh such as I had not known could be in me. There was something that thrilled me about the warped sweetness of Ronnie's features as he spoke. So thrilling, too, was the utter unlikelihood, as I believed, of those lips having ever in life befouled themselves with such a scurrilous phrase that the scene was invested for me with a perverse enchantment. I would replay it over and over in slow motion, so that every movement made by Ronnie's body would be ennobled by an ethereally glissading, 'harp-string' effect, would be decomposed, as it were, into a sequence of now graceful, now halting and shuddering, gestural spasms, each of them broken up in its turn by an alternating sequence of static frames.

As for *Tex-Mex*, it was no masterwork, to be sure, but its tale of the mutual hostility of two gangs of youths, and their nocturnal prowlings along the borderline dividing Texas from Mexico, proved absorbing enough in its ingenuous fashion. Ronnie played a member of the American gang, the offspring of 'white trash' drifters leading an idle, feckless existence in and out of sleazy saloon bars and the shabby caravan or 'mobile home' site that appeared to be their only residence. Pitted against them were the sons of illegal Mexican immigrant workers who were resented (rather unreasonably, as the film itself was mindful of pointing out, in a final sequence of revolting, speechifying mawkishness) for their readiness to accept just the kind of demeaning employment that the native-born *lumpenproletariat* would in any event have repudiated as being beneath even its tatterdemalion dignity.

Such, no doubt, was the earnest and simple-minded 'message' by which the film sought to justify its didactic pretensions, such was the message poor Ronnie so piously 'believed in', and it was one to which I myself would have been, in any other circumstance but this, utterly indifferent. Even here, it touched me only to the degree that its articulation had been prompted by the myriad indignities which the film's narrative heaped upon Ronnie's bruised and fragile little frame. For here, too, as I had so long ago divined would be the case, the actor had been cast – typecast, I would have said – as one of nature's victims, as one whose blood is meant for shedding, his body for gentle rape. Being the very youngest of the American gang, by whose more mature members he was treated as almost a mascot, it was he who would routinely bear the brunt of the Mexicans' aggression. And it was as well, in that closing scene, his death at their hands (by being held under the oily surface scum of a street fountain in the *louche* Mexican border town in which most of the action unfolded) that would bring about the eleventh-hour reconciliation of the two gangs, a reconciliation sanctified by the 'uplifting' rhetoric of a virile middle-aged priest who, as it would occur to me, seemed to devote suspiciously much of his energy to the welfare of these just post-pubescent parishioners (but whose motivations in this regard had been forearmed against such prurient speculation by the otherwise unexplainable shafts of light which chanced to fall on his permanently inclined head wherever he might happen to be). Mawkish it might be, but I had to own in spite of myself that I was moved (profoundly or superficially, what did it matter?) by the film's climax. I grew slowly conscious as I watched it of a queasiness in the pit of my stomach, a salty prickling of my eyelashes, a moistening under my eyelids as of rain dripping off a pair of tiny umbrellas, until the general blurriness of my vision confirmed to my amazement, when I drew myself up to switch off the recorder, that my commitment to

the drama – more precisely, to one of its participants –
had by the end become not only total but visible.

I would run and rerun these two precious tapes of mine
until scarcely a heartbeat was struck that I failed to
anticipate the instant before. A film viewed this many
times, I discovered, however mediocre may appear its
point of departure, must always end by acquiring unto
itself a special type of beauty, the beauty of things that
are or have come to seem *inevitable*. Each negligent and
certainly unrehearsed gesture, each fortuitous element to
have swum unsuspecting into the camera's ken – a face
in a crowd, a fleeting, half-glimpsed landscape, some
irrelevant, 'non-signifying' message just legible in a
drugstore window or on an extra's teeshirt – would by
the umpteenth viewing have been branded into the film's
textures, its grain, its very pores, as though all along its
producer or director had determined that it had to be so
and no other way, as though it were one of the cinema's
vocations, and perhaps its most elevated vocation, thus
to statufy spontaneity, to render the incidental indelible,
to hold the random to account.

And there was another discovery I would make, one
whose implications, as they penetrated, would startle me
most of all. I had permitted myself, no matter the whys
and wherefores, to take a close personal interest in one
young American film actor. In pursuance of that interest,
moreover, I had had to confine the parameters of my
field of operation to what was promptly and legitimately
available to a man in my position: which is to say, the
actor's appearances in just three films and the journalistic

coverage of his career in a collection of magazine articles and photographs. Even so, as I realised, with only such a meagre capital of information at my command, *I now knew more about Ronnie Bostock than about any other living individual.* Naturally, I continued to retain a modicum of scepticism with regard to the youth's publicly aired character and opinions, and had even let a few stronger doubts linger on as to certain uncorroborated and not easily credible details of his personal history. Yet it was by very virtue of their wellnigh unaltered reiteration from one article to the next, together with my own proven flair for reading between lines, that I was finally persuaded of the basic trustworthiness of my intelligence in the matter.

Therefore, proceeding from the broadest of canvases, I could claim to know the boy's age, his date and place of birth (San Fernando), his place of domicile (Chesterfield – apparently an almost entirely residential township on Long Island a few miles distant from the 'Hamptons' of such glamorous reputation), his family background and all other co-ordinates relating to his environment. I knew his height, his weight, the colour of his eyes and hair, the fact that he was very slightly myopic and that his skin tended to blister in the sun. I had studied photographs of him taken at successive stages of his physical development, from the classic snapshot of coddled infancy – of a tiny, quite unidentifiable seven-month-old baby laid out plump and naked on a patchwork coverlet and beaming at someone evidently not the photographer himself, as the infant's gaze was directed slightly to one side – to one of the very latest, of an unsmiling, humid-eyed Ronnie standing in a trellised garden, holding a rhubarb stalk in his hand. And, between these extremes, there had been summoned up, as though solely for my own fond and credulous attention, a pictorial chronology of Ronnie's progressive maturing. His face would start to lose its puppy fat (oh but, please God, not yet altogether). The form of his features, that stayed boyishly unsculpted throughout the earliest of the photographs, later ovalled out towards the chin. The childlike puffiness of his cheeks had quite suddenly retreated inward to expose the underpinning of his bone structure as well as the two diagonal shadows, like evening shades, that would fall aslant his face. His honey-hued hair, which had once draped his forehead with ringlets and kiss-curls, was then given its head, as it were, the left side upswung, the right allowed to tumble brow-wards in a curling forelock. His body, if still slight for someone of his age, acquired a perceptible curvature of the shoulders that some of the photographs had contrived to catch unawares. His hairless torso tautened and firmed. And his legs became frosted with a fine, wispy down, even if they had yet to forfeit the slender, stalky spindliness typical of the very late stages of adolescence.

Over the years Ronnie had lost weight, regained it, lost it again, put it on again. He was, self-admittedly, 'a pizza freak – with lots and lots of extra toppings!'. There was little that I did not now know of his taste in food, in clothes, in music, in girls, in sport, in movies and even in books (Stephen King, science-fiction and 'rock star biographies'). I knew that he had two tiny moles on his face, that his armpits were as clean of hair as a statue's, that the flat, shiny declivities behind his knees were as smooth as the palms of his hands, that the hair on the nape of his neck had been fetchingly shaped towards a receding point (except, in *Tex-Mex*, for a single wisp in the middle that curled down his collar like a stage Chinaman's pigtail, a style the boy, rather to my regret, had elected not to carry over into his private life). And I had watched the two films so often I knew exactly how Ronnie moved, how he would set one leg in front of the other when he walked, with what graceful turn of his body he would sit down or stand up or merely be quite motionless – for he had a lovely way all his own of just standing still.

There were, too, certain dormant aspects to his personality that the actor would expose through his publicity – indeed, could not help but expose. It had gradually come to my notice, for example, that among the several other young performers featured on the pages of the magazines there were some who appeared resolved to offer images of themselves rather less servile and sycophantic than his, less easily manipulated by the general house style. For one thing, their pin-ups were far less uniformly 'wholesome' than Ronnie's. They would be shown lounging against graffiti-streaked walls and in all manner of unsavoury settings, they would connive at drawing the eye towards haunched hips and shamelessly flaunted crotches and did not always smile for the photographer. In one interview an actor not any older than Ronnie, thuggishly good-looking yet with skin so taut and angular it looked almost flayed, a young tough if ever there was, made an offhand and only sulkily repentant allusion to his struggle against alcoholism; another, a little older, spoke of his dread of contracting

Aids; a third of his now faltering career. The pervasive ideology of these publications, the unreflecting and peculiarly American cult of *mens sana in corpore sano*, was not, then, bound to remain the immovable object it had once seemed to me, not at least if their young subjects could command the strength of character to resist it; and if Ronnie was unable or unwilling to assume any role other than that of the pretty ventriloquist's doll of those in whose interest it was to control his every movement, it could only be that he himself espoused that ideology without condition or else was lacking in just that strength of character. 'He is not very intelligent, there is not much on top,' I thought. 'He will only say what others have advised him to say.'

I started to reflect upon the race of actors, upon what a strange vocation indeed is that of the professional actor; it was a subject that had never preoccupied me in the past. At the very least, I concluded, the actor's intelligence must conform to a merely mechanistic model – a parody of true intelligence, in short, of a type that soon becomes impossible to distinguish from pure instinct. For, when he performs, what he is really performing is sums, sums inside his head, simple mental arithmetic, calculating from one instant to the next not only the range and intensity of those facial expressions destined for public consumption but also of those more latent embodiments of selfhood of whose precise importance to the delineation of character perhaps only the actor himself will ever be fully aware. It might be no more than the way in which his arms swing at his sides as he crosses a room or the precise stance of his feet even when the spectator is intent upon his smiling face. And there, too, when an actor smiles in a film, he must be able to call upon a whole panoply, a radiant bouquet, of smiles to select from, a file of smiles, so to speak – rueful, sly, sarcastic, ironic, sardonic, gentle, melancholic, whatever. So that the smile is made over into the portrait of a smile, the codified representation of a spontaneous initiative. And nothing could more conclusively demonstrate Ronnie's own undoubted insufficiency as a performer, yet nothing as well was more calculated to beguile his admirer, than the fact that when he smiled on the screen it was with his own unique and lovable smile, the smile I had come to know from dozens of snapshots, the only one he had. It was a document, not a representation, of a smile; one, moreover, that oftentimes seemed to me to have been eroded from within by a secret sorrow, as though the smiler were being ordered at gunpoint to 'Smile or else!' Thus would he open up his soul to view, make public property of his beauty and charm, his humour and tenderness, and only those more at ease applauding a statue than the living individual who had posed for that statue could ever think to reject such a priceless offering as second-best to one of those silvery, glib-tongued 'performances' which enable the actor to seek refuge in the role, to mask rather than shed light upon the recesses of his own nature. If Ronnie wore a mask, as was sometimes demanded of him, it was only the better to expose himself. For what is it, in effect, that may be regarded as the minimal, mundane but imperative condition of an actor's capacity to surprise us, to move us, to make us laugh, and so forth – whatever the desired object of his performance should happen to be? The answer, surely, is that he not be interchangeable, that his investment in a role be such as to cause any other actor in the same role to appear an *impostor*.

Thinking along these lines, recalling how my own existence had been transformed by Ronnie, I now clearly saw that if it be the actor's ultimate destiny to interpret, to serve as an interpreter between a mediated reproduction of living forms on the one hand and the world, the 'real' or unformalised world, on the other, if it be, simply but sublimely, his vocation to make us more alert to the latent strengths and frailties of our fellow men, then Ronnie Bostock, indifferent performer though he was, might be considered a great actor.

And again there came to my mind notions of representation, of what I had belatedly come to understand as the network of tensions underlying any cinematic representation of a human body, at once a recurrent icon of art history, a smooth, compliant, un-orificed vessel ready to be 'poured' into a series of poses, and a living, corporeal presence and identity.

Nakedness in art, I knew, was a matter of great complexity. A human body in representation, even in a work of pornography, is never naked, is always, in accordance with the art historian's celebrated distinction, 'nude'. Hence, because an actor performing to a film camera never ceases to present himself as being 'in character', the nudity he proffers up to the spectator's gaze is not that of his own body but belongs by rights, as would the costume he might wear in another scene, to the character he is playing. In none of his three films, of course, had Ronnie ever let himself appear naked, had only, in one scene of *Tex-Mex*, shown himself in a pair of low-cut sky-blue bathing-trunks. But were he ever to do so, then the self-exposure would again necessarily be of his own self, just as his smile was his own; it would, in a manner of speaking, advance *beyond representation*, it would make of his body the object not of a reproduction but of a regard. Since that nakedness had never been offered up, however, and remained a matter of pure speculation, my theory could not be tested; and, with a slight shudder, I realised that it was all there was left me, it was practically the last manifestation of Ronnie's being, whether in body or soul, that I had still to possess.

I was seated at my kitchen table, laid out for supper as usual by my housekeeper. I had not worked on my novel for some little while, nor even now, as blinking I rose once more to the surface of the external world, the world of real things and real people, did I contemplate doing so. I had been only half-consciously eating the curry which had been prepared for my supper; when I glanced down at the nearly empty plate, I discovered that the knife and fork were left untouched at its sides, that I had been picking at the meal with my fingers, stuffing it blindly into my mouth with such wholesale and indiscriminate relish that my lips still felt slobbery from stray scraps of chicken and rice and there were stains flecking the buttoned front of my grey woollen cardigan. I sensed that my face had fired up from my having eaten much too hastily, and I had an irresistible urge to blow my nose. I did so and, giving two or three luxuriantly violent snorts for good measure, recomposed my features. 'At my age,' I said to myself, then again softly, 'At my age!'

On the table, beside the plate that bore the smeary remains of my supper, my cuttings book lay open at a page on to which I had pasted one of Ronnie's most captivating pin-ups. The young actor was sitting backwards astride a chair, his arms resting along the slightly bevelled edge of the white formica chair-back, his shoulders curving forward to take his weight, his chin just brushing his splayed fingers. He had on a white shirt of a light, almost transparent cloth stippled with rows and rows of tiny dots, like perforations on a postage stamp, that somehow managed to appear of an even whiter whiteness than that of the shirt itself. The photograph had not perhaps been very expertly reproduced, for the two whitenesses, that of his shirt-front and that of the formica chair-back, all but dissolved into each other as I looked at them and I had to peer closely to see where one left off and the other began. It was also the imperfect quality of the reproduction, no doubt, that lent the boy's closed lips an improbably scarlet coloration, as though he were wearing lipstick. This was my own favourite photograph of Ronnie, had always been – and now, now, quite undone by the sway of my senses, I leaned over the table top, so far forward that my nose seemed on the point of grazing the page, and kissed him on his satiny paper lips. It had been a long courtship.

The following morning, a cold, sunny, reviving morning such as autumn sometimes holds in late reserve, I took a cab into Soho to one of the two newsagents' shops I had come to frequent. This was, unless there had been a shipping problem, the very day when I might expect to find the latest issue of *Teen Dream*. Behind the counter the turbanned Indian took impassive note of my appearance in the shop. I at once found the magazine I was looking for and glanced through its pages to assure myself of its contents. Then my eye started to stray to the shelf above, a shelf on which was displayed the shop's fairly extensive supply of pornography. On the covers of most of these magazines, which were nearly but not quite out of arm's reach, half-stripped, big-bosomed women, all of them as hard of feature and coarse of limb as naked barmaids, paraded their blowsy charms with repellent coyness. At the far end of the same shelf, however, the end closest the door, were two or three publications that I had already noticed, publications with such names as *Vulcan* and *Jupiter* and *Toy Boy*, concerning the nature of whose appeal, and the precise sexual orientation of whose readership, no ambiguity was possible. I stretched my arm up and, after a moment's hesitation, pulled down *Toy Boy*. On its cover stood a young man at the foot of an oak tree, his back to the camera, his head turned to face the purchaser with a gap-toothed but not unappealing grin on his craggy working-class features; as the ends of his undone belt hung loosely at his sides and the top of his jeans was sliding ever so slightly down his buttocks, I had the impression, as I was perhaps intended to, that the lad was urinating or about to urinate up against it. With a quick, covert glance at the newsagent, whose back happened to be turned away, I took a peek inside to make absolutely sure I knew what I was getting for my money – I had become a seasoned customer of clandestine literature and had no intention of being defrauded of my prize. A single glimpse of the inside sufficed: that which I was after was the first and indeed only thing to catch my eye on the page at which the magazine fell open in my hands.

I closed it again and prepared to take it with the other to the counter. But, even here, even now, I had not so anaesthetised myself to the opinion of the world to remain insensitive to the socio-moral niceties that the situation seemed to entail. Thus was I quite prepared to buy *Teen Dream*, prepared, too, to be seen buying a rag like *Toy Boy*, but some remaining shred of decency, of respect, respect for Ronnie, perhaps, rather than for myself, prevented me from buying the two of them together.

I replaced the more innocuous on the shelves. It was not that I was about to relinquish owning it altogether; I would purchase another copy separately, at the second newsagent's, a mere hundred yards away.

Once home, inside my study, its door locked, I read the article in *Teen Dream* that was devoted to Ronnie Bostock; read it as avidly as ever, even if, with the exception of a passing, teasing reference to 'a new and exciting movie that may just happen – but I'll only be uncrossing my fingers to sign the contract!!!' (not one of your own, I suspect, Ronnie dear), it turned out to be yet another recapitulative chronicle of the relatively few events of note, after all, actually to have taken place in the young man's life. Then I took a small pair of scissors from a desk drawer and started to cut along the outline of Ronnie's head in one of the three photographs which accompanied the article. It was his hairline that proved to be the greatest inconvenience, with each tuft, practically each strand, above the line of the forehead having to be snipped at with the utmost caution if I wished to produce a good likeness; equally, I was forced to take a few liberties with the jawline whose shadowy formlessness in the photograph had caused him, once it had been cropped, to appear unwantedly jowly. When I had completed it quite to my satisfaction, I performed the same operation on a second, smaller, monochromatic portrait. Then I picked them up, holding them in a gingerly way between my fingers so as not to crease them, removed *Toy Boy* from the plain brown envelope into which the newsagent had slipped it, and stepped over to the chaise-longue. Although it was not much after two o'clock in the afternoon, I drew the curtains together and switched on a small table lamp.

I extended myself on the chaise-longue, aligned my body on its right side, unfastened my belt and eased my trousers and underwear down past my knees. Trembling, as though I might at any instant call a halt to the whole loathsome, mad and degrading business, yet grimly getting on with it nevertheless, I set the pornographic magazine on the floor beneath me and started to turn its pages one by one. It had come to this. On each of these pages, filled as they were with naked male flesh (youthful but then again, I remarked, not always so very youthful flesh), filled as they were with young but not always so very young men posing salaciously in those settings that would seem to be the favoured preserve of homosexual fantasies (a beach, a swimming pool, a construction site), on each of the heads of these young men in turn, and depending on the size of the photograph or whether it was in colour or in black-and-white, I would place, hoping thereby to have the boy usurp then plausibly assume their diverse nudities, either one of the two little transposed heads of Ronnie Bostock. At the same time, I gently then more vigorously began to masturbate, rediscovering the long dormant cadences of solitary love and longing. But it happened that either the torso I had selected would be too beefy and muscular to carry with any real conviction Ronnie's still boyishly graceful features; or it would be too hollow-chested, too hirsute, too bony, too squat, too tall, too short, even too horribly tattooed; or the photographic perspectives failed to correspond properly, the respective grains proved impossible to reconcile, the dissimilarities in contrast and definition were too great; or else the slant of Ronnie's head was so out of line with that of some young bruiser's body he looked almost as though he were being throttled. Even in the single instance where (if I half-closed my eyes) head and body were fairly reasonably matched – the photograph was of a rather exotically complexioned, heavy-lidded youth sitting naked and hunched on an incongruously chintzy sofa, his slim, hairless legs bent at the knees and gaping apart at the thighs and the toes of his two bare feet curling around the hemline of the sofa's cushions – whoever this hybrid creature was, it was manifestly not Ronnie. And it never, never would be Ronnie, I knew, as in sheer impotence and despair I hurled the filthy magazine from my sight. It would always be a fraud, a low and disgusting confidence trick that I had tried to play against myself!

Overtaken by swift remorse and unable to tolerate my ridiculous half-dressed state a second longer, I stood up and adjusted my clothes. I knew now that, if ever I was to draw the poison, there was only one course left to be taken. It is, paradoxically, logic that is the mainspring of every obsession: advancing measure by measure, step by single step, not one of them skipped or leapt over, towards the psychic acrostics of madness itself, such is the path taken, usually consentingly, by the obsessive. By the repulsive charade to which I had just allowed myself to be party, I had attempted to leap over a crucial step and circumvent the logic in whose adamantine machinery I had become enmeshed. But I had also come to know what the next step must be, indeed I must have known it all along, and I stood at the window with my hands folded behind my back in a pose suggestive of some newly won mood of serenity and of a calm and deliberate acceptance of what was to be.

Eager though I was to be off, I was retained in the city by affairs both literary and practical for some ten days after my decision had been taken; during which time I bought a round-trip 'plane ticket for New York and alerted my housekeeper to the likelihood that I would be out of London for a lengthy and, until I knew better, open-ended period. I read through what I had written of *Adagio*, placed the manuscript inside a folder and locked it away in the desk drawer that already contained my album of cuttings. Then, on a day between the middle and end of November, and without advising my agent or indeed any other person of my departure, I boarded my 'plane at Heathrow.

If, as I have said, I was fairly widely travelled, this happened to be my very first visit to America, a continent which had never held much interest or allure for me. It was also my first extended trip anywhere for a number of years and only the second time I had flown – and it was not, all things considered, the most agreeable of experiences. I fretted at the fact alone that the aircraft's first-class section was full, its every seat occupied by dynamic young executives, as I assumed them to be, each of them – sitting in pin-striped shirt-sleeves, balancing some company report on his knees and dreamily and interminably clicking a ballpoint pen – as indistinguishable from his fellows as though all of them were Japanese. I did no more than nibble on the wretched meals the stewardesses would tirelessly set before me. Although (as one for whom the cinema had of late assumed a significance that it had never known before) I raised my eyes from time to time to contemplate the soundless posturing of the bland and blurred forms that drifted across the small cabin screen just in front of me, it was with a gesture of tetchy impatience that I motioned away the offer of a side-order of earphones. And during the slow, solitary hours spent crossing the ocean I fell prey to the worst of the traveller's anxieties. Why, I would ask myself, *why was I here*, why flying off to an unknown destination in quest of some as yet not satisfactorily formulated personal craving – one that, if it were ultimately to be satisfied, would lead to nothing else but my having got Ronnie Bostock 'out of my system'? I knew I could not legitimately hope for more than that yet at the same time I had no wish to be cured, to be restored, to recover my self-possession. I knew equally

99

well that, no matter what the final outcome would be, no matter that all the odds were against the success of my mission, I would never permit myself to return empty-handed.

I had not consciously tried to sleep, but I found myself awakened, as the aircraft was already making a banked descent towards Kennedy Airport, by the sound of an amplified male voice announcing that we were flying directly over Long Island. I sleepily roused myself and peered out of the tiny cabin porthole. There, spread out beneath me, only slightly obscured from my view by drifts of cobwebby cloud that were attenuated almost to the point of transparency, there, somewhere amid that peaceful quiltwork of half-rural, half-suburban America, perhaps in one of those neatly aligned little settlements of red-roofed, white-walled houses or else, more likely, in one of the larger residences set down on its own in green parkland and from which there would come a flash of translucent blue, the blue, I had no doubt, of a swimming-pool – somewhere down there was where Ronnie lived and where I myself was fated to go. And the wear and tear on my system that this knowledge produced struggled with the reckless exultation of my heart.

My arrival into New York passed off without incident. The airport's customs and immigration inspection turned out to be neither gruelling nor protracted, not at any rate the ordeal I had expected it to be. I immediately found a taxi ready to bear me off to my hotel; I dutifully gave myself up to admiring the city's incomparable and (it being late in the afternoon) now half-illuminated skyline; then my coal-black cabdriver was ploughing and plunging through the vertiginous canyons of 'downtown' Manhattan.

It was my hotel, however, located exactly halfway between Fifth and Sixth Avenues, that did not at all meet my expectations. It had been recommended to me many years before by one of my Cambridge friends – my wife and I had been planning an American tour, that had had to be cancelled when she was suddenly stricken with the illness of which she was shortly thereafter to die – and he had expatiated with some warmth on its decaying splendour and the solid old-fashioned virtues of its service. But what I was to discover when I entered the lobby could be called decayed only in reference to taste: a long, split-level foyer whose lower-level bar area was laid out in a sickly spectrum of beiges and apricots, its chairs and low tables all with arms and legs of tubular steel and speckled black cushions which looked from where I was standing like so many enormous blackcurrent pastilles. The style, too, of my own suite I immediately recognised as being merely an extension of that of the lobby. Its apricot-and-black lavatory or 'bathroom' in particular made me think – as I could not resist remarking to the bellboy who accompanied me, a dark-haired, prettified young man rendered all the more effeminate by having been obliged to sport a suit of hyper-virile black leather livery – of 'a bathroom in Hell'. At this comment the young bellboy, to my amusement, could not have appeared more crestfallen than if it were he himself who had been responsible for designing the fittings. But just as suddenly he grinned again (exposing what looked to be a tiny jade earring that he had had in some manner clipped on to the upper rim of one of his front teeth) and, as though personally to bear on his shoulders the city's reputation for smart repartee, replied, 'Maybe, though, that's why Hell *is* Hell – because it doesn't have a bathroom.' He chuckled at his own joke, which he seemed also, thoughtfully, to be storing away in his mind for a more promising occasion.

On my putting the question to him, he informed me that the hotel had only the year before been purchased by an international consortium (here, presumably to convey the vast sums of money this consortium had had at its disposal, he slyly rubbed one thumb and forefinger together), which then had had it completely renovated. While he chattered away, I scrutinised him cynically, thinking to myself, 'He really is an American Felix Krull,' and wondering whether his duties would necessarily cease at the bedroom door. As he turned to leave, I pressed a dollar bill into the palm of his open hand and watched him sashay along the hallway towards the lift.

That evening I strolled out into the streets of the city in search of some suitable restaurant and almost at once found myself in Times Square. I was exhausted and out of sorts, my eyes smarted as though the pupils had been scraped with sandpaper, my ears revolted at the pandaemonium of police and ambulance sirens, screeching tires and endlessly gabbling pedestrians that filled the heavy-scented night air. I was more confused than delighted by the hurry and flurry of New York, by all its noise and neon. I was assailed by nameless fears and began to suspect everyone whose path I crossed of hoping to pick my pockets.

Suddenly, before I knew what had happened, I was

waylaid by an outlandishly tall, pot-bellied black man, barefoot and shirtless, his left ear caked with congealed blood, his right ear missing and in its stead something ghastly, something without form, as obscene and grotesque and misshapen as an ear, were an ear not just an ear. He lumbered towards me, gripped me by the lapels of my overcoat and kept muttering the same demented sentence between his teeth and into my face, a sentence of which all I could make out was the reiterated, ritualised salutation: 'Hey, man . . . Hey, man . . . Hey, man . . . Hey, man . . .' In his right hand he held a half-consumed hot dog nestling in wads of greasy paper and dripping with mustard that looked like soft diarrhoea, but it was with his left, in a to-and-fro motion, that he tugged viciously at my coat lapels, and I recoiled with a shudder from every foul blast of a breath that smelled of some unholy compound of whisky and fried onions. This lasted some minutes, until I panicked altogether, pulled myself free at last and with the sound of rumbling, mocking laughter behind me took to my heels.

By an excruciatingly roundabout route, that somehow involved my walking down much of Broadway, I managed to find my way back to the hotel. Still quite haggard and shaken, smoking cigarette after cigarette, I ordered myself some scrambled eggs in my suite and immediately afterwards went to bed.

The next morning, after sleeping myself out, I felt very much invigorated. Manhattan was cold and sparkling. A beautiful city, unquestionably – I would have to explore it one day. In the meantime, it was with a light step, with the hotel's street map in my gloved hand, that I directed my path towards Grand Central Station.

There, at a small information booth, I learned that trains for Suffolk County, the area of Long Island in which Chesterfield apparently was situated, did not depart from Grand Central at all but Penn Central, a station of which I had had no prior knowledge. But even if this small setback was to cause me a moment's frustration, the mere fact of hearing the name of Ronnie's town uttered as though it were a community like another, a community with nothing at all mythic or unattainable about it, the reality of whose existence could not have asked for vindication more unequivocal than to be reflected in something as mundane and authoritative as a railway timetable, buoyed me up immeasurably. Chesterfield existed, and Ronnie lived there; therefore Ronnie, too, existed and he could be approached like any other individual living anywhere else.

Such were my reflections as I made my way back through the station's subterranean halls out towards the sunlit exit. And it was when still underground, in one of those same marble halls, that I chanced to notice a large newsagent's shop, in which, it occurred to me, I might buy an English newspaper. I stepped in. Before I had had a chance to enquire about the possibility, my eye was attracted to one rack in particular, along which were shelved dozens, possibly even scores, of the teen magazines I had become addicted to, only a handful of which were ever sold in England at all and those at least two or three weeks after they went on sale in New York.

To have chanced upon such a treasure trove! There was an article on Ronnie in virtually all of them, and even if the purpose of my visit to America was precisely to supercede what I hoped I would one day look back at as a pathetic and primitive stage of my love affair with the youth, I picked each one up with a trembling hand and the manic, feverish trepidation of one in a dream, excitedly examined its contents then laid it aside with the others I intended to buy.

Finally, I had in my hands what must have been the newest of all, since the publication date on its cover actually postdated that very day and month. I turned its pages to the article on Ronnie, and I had just time to register the fact that the photograph which illustrated it, and which itself was garlanded by a pair of pink ribboned hearts and two little sets of wedding bells, was of Ronnie clasping hands with an unknown young woman, and that its caption read 'Ronnie B's Secret Engagement!!!' – when, my heart throbbing, I felt the pile of magazines sliding one by one down my overcoat on to the floor, started to gasp for breath, swayed and an instant later lost consciousness.

When I came to, I heard, as though through some sort of lead piping, the question 'Are you okay?' Someone, who would turn out to be the newsagent himself, a burly shirt-sleeved man in late middle age, chewing on the half-smoked stump of a cigar, was assisting me to my feet. I had fainted. The newsagent was asking me if he should fetch a doctor. Out of my anxiety to play down the incident I contrived to draw myself away from him with an officious and quite unintended brusqueness. 'I feel quite well,' I murmured, steadying myself against the shop counter. 'Please don't trouble anyone.' 'Well, frankly,' said the newsagent, scrutinising me, 'to me you look terrible – but if you say you're okay, then I guess you're okay. Have a nice day.' And he returned to his place behind the counter.

It took a few minutes for me to pull myself together. Without attending to which order they ought to be in, I hurriedly replaced on the shelves all the magazines but the one that had brought me the dreadful news. I was still trembling when I paid for it and, although I mumbled an inaudible thank you, I endeavoured not to look my puzzled Samaritan straight in the face. I walked only a few steps along the corridor outside, stopped, then, casting a nervous glance on either side of me, opened the magazine and read the article through.

That which, even as I swooned, I had half attempted to persuade myself could yet simply be mere journalistic hyperbole, a publicity stunt, an unscrupulous ruse to sell more copies than some rival publication, there it was, in black-and-white, incontrovertibly true. For nearly three months now, the very three months of my own passion for him, Ronnie had been secretly engaged to be married. His fiancée was named Audrey. She was twenty-three years old, three years older than he, a fashion model of, to my eye, nondescript physical appearance, and she and Ronnie had met in Hollywood where she was 'filming a series of Pepsi commercials'. The 'new and exciting movie' that had been titillatingly referred to in *Teen Dream* was – oh Ronnie, how could you! – *Hotpants College III*. Filming would start in six weeks and it was the young couple's intention to be married on Long Island then immediately afterwards fly out to California for the shoot; and Ronnie would carry his bride over the threshold of the luxurious new condominium awaiting them in the Hollywood Hills. They were young, as they knew, very young, but Ronnie trusted sincerely that his many fans would understand, for 'when you're as crazy in love as we are, there's really no point in hanging on.'

I closed the magazine. I felt a sickening taste on the lid of my mouth, the taste of emptiness, the sterile taste of nothing at all. Salty tears sprang into my eyes. 'Only six weeks!' I muttered to myself in a febrile voice as I strode along the corridor. 'Six weeks – there's no time to be lost!'

One or two of those passers-by whose paths I crossed would turn to glance at this strange individual in their midst; not many, though, for New Yorkers have grown accustomed to seeing strangers talk to themselves in public places.

Almost as though the self-injunction that there was no time to be lost must take immediate effect, I hastened out of Grand Central Station. For a long moment, I stood staring at the meshed, lattice-like grid of the city's numbered streets and avenues on the map I had taken with me from my hotel; then frantically dashed off in what I trusted was the direction of Madison Square Garden (the same Madison Square Garden where Ronnie had once attended a Michael Jackson concert), deep in whose nether regions, assuming I had not misread the map, Penn Central should be found.

So it turned out; trains were relatively frequent, and the very next one was due to leave nearly at once. I purchased a return ticket and set off for Chesterfield.

A little over two hours later I stepped down from the train to find myself – precisely nowhere. The station was certainly that of Chesterfield, yet, outside and around it, apart from a highway, a lonely, seemingly unattended garage and, to the west, its cold aluminium glitter turning silverish in the early afternoon sun, what might have been a modestly sized power station, there appeared not a sign of human commerce or habitation. The railway station, too, was quite deserted save for myself – for I was alone among the train's passengers to have alighted at Chesterfield – and an elderly black hunchback who was sweeping it out. From him I learned that the town itself was 'jest a way 'long the highway there'; and that although, yes, it was well within walking distance, 'no one ever do walk'.

The walk into Chesterfield took me forty minutes. To begin with, and for a long time, the landscape remained as characterless as that by which I had been greeted on my arrival. Then, very gradually, came the first feelers of the community ahead: a graveyard sloping gracelessly down towards the highway, every tombstone in it white and new, as though the townspeople had only just started to die; a quite unpicturesque lumber mill with an Alsatian dog asleep among the shavings; the first of the town's private residences, of which only the driveway was visible and a gatepost in the form of an ornate, cod-mediaeval parchment. And suddenly, almost as I was about to give up hope of ever arriving there, the township of Chesterfield, Ronnie's town, reared up to meet me.

In England it might not have been judged a town at all. The 'city center', as the locals were rather grandly given to calling its municipal and commercial area, was intersected by but two sets of parallel boulevards travers-ing each other at right angles in the manner of a game of noughts-and-crosses; when each of these reached the edge of the town proper, it would continue on up into the rolling forested uplands within whose snug, soft dale the community lay, and it was there that most of its residents had built their homes. Chesterfield, in short, was a tolerably charming specimen of affluent American suburbia, not too arch, not too daintified, its restaurants and shops (there was even a lone gun store, as I remarked, forefronted by an eye-catchingly symmetrical, evidently window-dressed display of rifles and revolvers) encased in a pleasant reddish-brown brick, its trio of banks flanked by their own trim shrubbery like miniature mansions, its exclusively residential streets, along which I roamed after having explored the centre of the town itself, bordered by neat and mostly unostentatious clapboard houses with freshly painted white picket fences and perhaps a child's tricycle parked outside the front door. A certain faint tanginess in the air and the distant screech of a gull helped to remind me that I was indeed on an island of sorts, but there was not a hint of the fey and raffish romanticism of that Long Island of Fitzgeraldian myth.

On this first day, although I rejoiced in the sensation that everywhere I walked Ronnie must have walked before me, that now at last we were, in an expression he himself had employed in one of his interviews, *sharing the same space*, and although (preposterously, as I acknowledge) I was already bracing myself, keeping myself on wellnigh constant alert, for the miracle of a chance encounter, my overriding concern was to find a place where I might stay on and plan my strategy.

Towards the latter part of the afternoon, realising that I had not eaten all day, I ordered a cheeseburger in a small, clean, noisy diner whose wooden booths with their studded leather upholstery lent it a vaguely nineteen-twentyish air. Its proprietor and chef was one Irving Buckmuller, and his sole error of taste and judgment – for the cheeseburger itself, to my knowledge the first I had ever eaten in my life, turned out to be quite delicious – was the name he had inflicted on his establishment: *Chez d'Irv*.

Irving himself, fat and slovenly, with a great football of a head that was exactly the same shape as his torso, would regularly emerge from his kitchen wiping huge pancake hands on a filthy, once-white apron and wafting into the restaurant along with him a billow of stale lukewarm steam. With a kind of foul-mouthed joviality he would make his round of the booths, leaning right over his customers' shoulders and enquiring in a gravelly voice, that sounded as though his vocal chords had been removed, whether everything was to their satisfaction. He seemed to take an especial interest in me, as he would have done, no doubt, in any new and unfamiliar patron; and, ignoring his waitress's strident appeals for 'one eggs over easy' and 'two blue-plate specials, hold the relish', settled himself down on the seat opposite my own, told me of how he had been based in Aldershot during the Second World War and asked if I had ever come across his 'best British buddy' of those days, a certain Ben Sutcliffe. I was longing in my turn to ask Irving if he was acquainted with Ronnie Bostock, was suddenly, absurdly, panic-stricken lest my motive be made immediately apparent and confined myself to an anodyne query about local hotels. There was only one, I learned, a 'motel court' on the outskirts of the town, and when I had finally succeeded in disengaging myself from the chef's bearlike conviviality I made my way there. It was a matter of a few minutes to reserve myself a modest semi-detached bungalow and pay the fawning proprietress for a week's lodging in advance. I returned to New York by the next train, passed a second night in my hotel (a night full of churning dreams in which I would drift back and forth between scenes of great violence – violence whose precise source remained for me wholly unlocatable – and a sense of physical and spiritual well-being of a sweetness so indescribable, so all-encompassing, as to defy comparison with any of my life's moments of intensest rapture) and checked out early the next morning. Then I returned to Chesterfield.

It would be tedious to narrate in any detail or with any respect for their chronology my movements during the next ten days or so. I had made the trip to Long Island with, as I imagined, a 'plan', only to have it dawn on me, once there, that I had no plan, as that word is understood, only an impromptu and unreasoned resolve to confront Ronnie face to face. But how was I to go about it? My first instinct was quite simply to consult the telephone directory which I found (alongside an ancient Gideon Bible that had, as its bookmark, a tattered, comically dated pornographic postcard) in the top drawer of the bedside desk in my motel room. There was, needless to say, no Ronnie Bostock listed for Chesterfield – no Bostock at all, in fact, appeared to live in Suffolk County. In itself that initial and not exactly unforeseeable drawback offered scant cause for alarm:

terrified of being laid seige to by his more rapacious fans, Ronnie would certainly have asked to be assigned an ex-directory number. Yet it had the effect of clouding my brain with fresh anxieties. What, I said to myself, what if the boy, as would be all too likely, were at this very moment in Hollywood discussing his new project, or what, instead, if he were merely holidaying somewhere – in England, perhaps, in *London*! – or what if it were simply not true that he lived in Chesterfield, what if all those cretinous magazines had been conspiring from the very start to throw his admirers off the scent, what then? I sweated in horror at the notion, not that I might have come so far for nothing, but that I might eventually have to return, and then live on, live on as before, without ever having known Ronnie, and I· determined that it would not be so.

As a means of learning his address, I briefly and vainly flirted with the possibility of bribing the town's only postman, whose route would sometimes cross my own, the two of us being alike and unique in our obligation, albeit for different reasons, to prowl the streets of Chesterfield at all hours of the day. It was now just under a week away from December, and there had come since my arrival days of heavy rainfall and even sleet when I would nevertheless feel compelled to leave the motel in the morning and spend every daylit hour in the pursuit of my prey. Thus would I walk along one of the streets in the town until I arrived at its first set of traffic lights; at these take a left or right turning and continue until this second street be traversed in its turn by a third; when I would alter direction yet again and now walk right to the circumference of the township itself. This was what I thought of as the inner circuit, in the course of which I would very thoroughly cover the shopping area, peer in at the frosted, already Christmassy windows of coffee shops, wander as though aimlessly along the aisles of supermarkets, find myself purchasing some useless and valueless geegaw in a haberdasher's store whose over-decorated windows would not permit me to ascertain from outside exactly who might be within. But there was also the outer circuit, when I would saunter up the quiet residential streets sloping calmly into the surrounding uplands, streets that were usually quite deserted save for a group of children playing baseball on a front lawn or a lone angler bearing on his shoulder all his insectlike tackle. Here, patiently, from one house to the next, I looked out for some clue or other bearing upon the householder's identity, a clue that was all the harder to detect in that I had absolutely no conception of what it might amount to.

An ever-constant dread was that I would become conspicuous, that the honest townspeople of Chesterfield would come to notice and set to wondering about the alien, solitary figure who appeared to have no legitimate business in the town other than that of merely walking, to and fro, day in and day out, among its inhabitants. But although I strove to pass unnoticed, to efface myself in the bustle, it happened that, except at one particular hour late in the forenoons of weekdays and again during the whole of the afternoons of the two weekend days, there was very seldom to be seen milling along the pavements of the shopping streets the sort of harassed and yet high-spirited family crowd by which an English equivalent of Chesterfield would have been enlivened on an almost daily basis. And I felt sure that the presence of the lone, brooding foreigner that I must have appeared – the heavy, stolid grey of whose overcoat, moreover, stood out against the bright, childishly primary colours of the windcheaters and anoraks sported by most of the locals and by which the contented and uncomplaining race of Americans succeed in disowning winter's very existence – had already begun to attract inquisitive comment.

I lunched every day in Irving's diner, where my cool, non-committal reserve about the purpose of my visit to Chesterfield had finally stanched my host's amiable garrulity; no more than a gruffly discreet 'G'afternoon' would we exchange whenever Irv made one of his steam-enhaloed irruptions into the dining area. And, by the late afternoon when hope had had to be abandoned for that day, or else even earlier did I feel too tired and discouraged to prolong the operation, I would retire into my little bungalow and on most evenings watch television.

It was there, in front of the desultorily flickering screen in my sitting-room, that an idea came to me, an idea so simple it could not conceivably be so, but so audacious it just might. I burrowed into my suitcase, in the depths of which, underneath unpacked linen, I had stowed away the magazine bearing news of Ronnie's impending marriage. I opened it at the page in question and let my eyes skim through the article until at last they saw what they were looking for: the surname of Ronnie's fiancée. Then I turned to the telephone directory on my bedside table, sought the letter L and ran my finger down a column until I found, afforded almost hallucinatory prominence by the ridge of my now slightly grubby and unmanicured fingernail, the entry: *Lynn, Audrey, 16 Jefferson Hill, Ches.*

I paced up and down the little room, triumphant in possession of a clue at last and feeling as though, having secured this one piece of information, I had crossed a second Atlantic. But if I could scarcely contain my delight at the fact that the young woman's telephone number had all the time been listed in the Suffolk County directory and that the telephone itself was within easy reach of my arm, I did not dial the number; another, very much more effective, course lay open to me.

Next morning I made directly for Jefferson Hill. As I vaguely recalled from my perambulations, it was one of those residential streets outlying the town centre. Each of the houses along it being spacious in itself and enclosed on every side by its own rambling grounds, no. 16, which I could remember already having passed more than once, was located some little distance into the countryside. It was not one of the larger of the houses, but its saffron-yellow clapboard walls and the roofed-over porch that ran the length of its façade made it appear old and nostalgic and cottagey. There were blinds down on its two front windows. As I slowly, self-consciously, passed in front of it that first time, I observed that there was, on its right side, just visible to a passer-by, a small and overgrown trellised garden – without question the same one in which Ronnie had once been so memorably photographed! Then, too, on the left side, I sighted an open garage, its mechanically operated door tilting half-upwards and outwards; and, parked within, a glossy powder-blue sports car, a Porsche. What caused my heart on sight of it to beat even faster was not just the implication that someone, evidently, was at home. In my photograph album, I could not quite recall where, there was a snapshot of a beaming Ronnie framed in the window of just such a motor car; the snapshot was in colour and the car – the car was powder-blue. *It was Ronnie's car.* Shaking with excitement, I made a swift mental note of the first three letters of its registration number, enough, I believed, for my immediate purpose.

There was nothing to be done for the instant but to pass on – I did not dare to show myself hanging about so on the street. I walked to the top of the hill just before it dipped again to enter the surrounding forest. It was that little summit, in fact, that seemed to demarcate the outer circumference of the town. By a stroke of great fortune for me, there was no habitation of any kind further out (unless one counted the odd isolated house in the hills), just hedgeless, uncultivated meadowland on one side, the forest on the other. From such a vantage point I would have a satisfactory view of every coming and going at no. 16 but it would be most unlikely if I were to be spotted in my turn; and were a car ever to approach me from either direction, then I would feign close interest, as might anyone out for a casual stroll, in some unusual roadside plant or shrub.

The vigil could well be long. Of all the humiliations I had heaped upon myself in the cause of my passion this, I knew, was quite the most ridiculous and grotesque, and risky – added to which, it might even prove to be ultimately fruitless. But I had come too far and was now too close to satisfying my ambition to let myself be prejudiced by the mean-spirited politics of the common-sense cast of mind.

It was, in fact, a few minutes before three on that same day that it happened. The front door of no. 16 opened and Audrey appeared on the threshold. Even from my observation post I had no doubt at all that it was she. From where I spied upon her I saw that she wore slacks, a cape in a sombre tartan-like material, and was hatless. She turned the key in the lock and briskly walked over to the garage, at which point she disappeared from my view. After a moment the Porsche started to ease down the driveway, turned to the right, townwards, and drove off out of sight.

I immediately quitted my post and, half-walking, half at a run, set off in the same direction, down the hill towards Chesterfield. I slackened my pace only when passing in front of no. 16, for I couldn't countenance the risk of being observed moving at a speed unseemly for a man of my age and carriage. It was also my intention once more to run an eye over its façade. But nothing seemed to be stirring from within the house, which, when I reminded myself that Audrey had locked its front door behind her, was only what I ought to have expected.

On reaching the shopping precinct, I hunted in a fever this way and that, hunted like a dog that has been separated from its master, rushed from restaurant to bank, from bank to supermarket, in an ever more forlorn hope that the powder-blue Porsche would be sitting parked outside. I searched everywhere, thought even to explore a few of the other residential streets along the outer perimeter in case she might be paying a visit to some local acquaintance, but in the end found myself cheated – the car was nowhere to be seen. Panting, quite unnerved, guessing that Audrey had most probably gone driving into East Hampton, I was forced to abandon my search for the day and wearily returned to the motel.

Later that evening, though, in a break with the routine that had now become almost second nature to me, I chose again to walk alone through Chesterfield's lamplit streets – all now entirely deserted, save for two half-empty restaurants – and found myself drawn on as though by chance to Jefferson Hill. I walked past no. 16. One of the three upstairs windows was illuminated; the garage door was closed.

It is likely that, in my haunted state of mind, I should not for too long have been capable of keeping up my vigil and been driven to some drastic and even irrevocable act of precipitation; but providence elected to favour my cause sooner than I could ever have hoped for. There was no trace of Ronnie himself in the house on Jefferson Hill. But three times after the incident I have described (two of these on a single day), while standing watch I had seen Audrey step outside, walk to the garage and drive away in the Porsche; and three times had I followed her in vain, red-faced and maddened with frustration. On the fourth occasion, however, arriving breathless and sweating in the centre of town, I all but stumbled upon the car in the parking space of a small supermarket a mere two doors away from Irving's diner.

This was the moment of truth. I could not turn back. The very idea of fumbling or declining to seize the opportunity that now presented itself to me was unendurable. I had to go on.

I entered the supermarket. Near its entrance was a row of shopping chariots whose metal frames were neatly imbricated one within the next like staples in a stapling machine. I pulled one out for myself and, walking along the cool and colourful aisles, began to load it up with tins of processed vegetables, packets of breakfast cereals, stringy little netfuls of radishes and beet, indiscriminately and hardly paying attention to what I was about, my only care being to sight my quarry. There were few shoppers at that hour of day, most of them young mothers with their offspring straddling their chariots' little top-trays, and I did not have any difficulty catching up with Audrey.

Wearing a none too clean pair of jeans and a zippered black leather jerkin, she was strolling in a loose, slantwise fashion dead ahead of me. Every so often she would draw up at one of the shelves, take down a tin of something or other, turn it over in her hands – from her neck, I remarked, hung a pair of horn-rimmed glasses which she would prop on her nose when inspecting a label – and either replace it or drop it into her chariot. Then walked on, I just a few steps behind her.

We continued thus for several minutes more, Audrey moving at her own easy, loitering pace, I watchfully keeping my distance, waiting only for the chance to make my play yet also wondering whether, if such a chance were to arise, I would have the nerve to take advantage of it. And, almost at once, it did arise. For, when Audrey turned a corner, I momentarily lost sight of her; and then, following after, I saw that she had just left her chariot unattended in the centre of the aisle and paused to bend over a long, low deep-freeze cabinet.

I braced myself for what I knew to be the impending moment, the now unstayable moment, of crisis and climax; I watched her as she lifted out of the freezer a cellophane-wrapped chicken and seemed to weigh it in her two hands; then, as though gone utterly mad, I grasped the cross-handle of my own chariot and sent it recklessly careening towards hers.

The two vehicles janglingly collided. Audrey, still holding the chicken in her hand, turned, startled, to see me standing there. But I, too, feigning to notice only now what had occurred, contrived on the instant to turn around from the shelves of dairy products to which I had just to all outward intents and purposes been directing my attention.

As I darted forward to extricate the two entangled chariot handles, I could not have been more profuse in apologies, more unmistakably British equally in manner and accent; and Audrey, whom the little incident had initially irritated – that it was so was visible enough on her features – now relaxed and let herself be charmed.

Doubtless, I said, blushing inwardly at my own mendacity, I had made an awkward movement which caused me to back off into my trolley. It was unforgivable of me to be so clumsy and – but (I gazed intently into her face) surely she and I had met before? Audrey stiffened at this, which she patently suspected of being an improper overture, and all the more reprehensible in that it had been made by so improbable a masher. She gave a curt shake of the head and prepared to turn away. But although such a slight would once have chilled me to the marrow, and still made my heart painfully contract, I was by now a past master in the crafts of deception and felt myself to be impregnable. Why no, no, no, of course not, I went on, at first haltingly then with greater self-confidence, indeed, we had never met, it was quite simply that I recognised her from a photograph I had recently been shown. A photograph? So it was that I 'explained' my error – and even though I had been tirelessly rehearsing it in my motel room, the explanation was something of a *tour de force* all the same.

I had, I explained, a godchild, a delightful eleven-year-old girl whom I enjoyed spoiling with birthday and Christmas gifts and invitations to the cinema and to tea at the Ritz. In London, naturally. Now this young darling – her name, by the way, was Alice – had one very favourite actor whose photographs she would obsessively clip out of fan magazines and whose films she had seen many times over. Yes, a now smiling and visibly relieved Audrey had already guessed the name of my godchild's hero. I went on. A few days before leaving London – I had travelled as far as Long Island to complete my new novel untempted by the capital's pleasures and distractions – I was a writer, yes – I had found little Alice quite woebegone. The poor thing had just learned that her idol was not for very much longer to be the 'eligible bachelor-about-town' she worshipped from afar, and she had shown her godfather that snapshot of Ronnie and Audrey together that had blighted her childish dreams.

My tale, amusing, also rather sad in its way, and well told, enchanted Audrey and convinced her of the blamelessness of my purpose in engaging her in conversation.

Embarrassed at having harboured such an unmerited suspicion, she cordially accepted my proffered hand and introduced herself. We went on strolling side by side, chatting congenially if still a little hesitantly, each of us in turn removing an item from off the shelves – indeed, so generously on my own part that when we reached the checking-out counter I discovered that I had encumbered myself with a chariot-load of groceries nearly as bountiful as hers.

It was at the counter that, having first carefully prepared the terrain, I started to speak of Ronnie himself, of *Tex-Mex* and *Skid Marks* (I couldn't bring myself to mention *Hotpants College II*), which I claimed to have seen when accompanying my godchild to the cinema. To be sure (I smoothly countered a mild protest on Audrey's part), these were films hardly destined for someone like myself. And yet I had been impressed, most impressed, by Ronnie's performances, I detected in them a physical presence and an emotional intensity that the somewhat impoverished material was not best designed to turn to account.

As a glowing Audrey nodded her head ever more vigorously, in agreement with opinions she herself had beyond a doubt voiced more than once, I passed on to the way in which Ronnie on film would appropriate the space around him, his nimble-footed yet slightly crabwise gait, his timorous yet somehow defiant stance; I spoke of the youthful skittishness of the character he played in *Tex-Mex* and how it rendered for me the scene of his death all the more poignant; of his potential range and depth as a performer, which in my own view had as yet been underexploited. And if it would have struck a

wholly rational intelligence that there might be something suspect and not altogether plausible in an
English writer in his late middle age holding such strong
and well-informed opinions about a young, virtually
unknown American actor – even a writer with, as I
heard myself shamelessly claim, not a few important
connections in the British film industry – Audrey was
simply too dazed by my speech to let it be marred by
scepticism.

We left the supermarket together, I laden with not
merely my own bulging carrier bag but also with
Audrey's, of which I had insisted on relieving her, and
strolled across the empty car park to the powder-blue
Porsche. If I failed now, I knew, it might be all up for
me, for I could not tolerate the idea of renewing my
surveillance of Jefferson Hill.

'And – and where is Ronnie these days?' I enquired.

'In L.A.,' was the reply. 'He's due back day after
tomorrow.'

'Ah, indeed . . .' I said, the outwardly unruffled tone
of my voice belied, if for no one but myself alone, by a
wild flutter in my heart. 'Then perhaps you'd convey the
very best wishes of an admirer – or, should I say, two
admirers. I refer to my godchild,' I added with an insipid
smile.

Audrey nodded pleasantly and seemed on the point of
taking her leave of me. I could not yet let her go. 'Or
perhaps,' I went on to suggest, 'I might convey them in
person.' I planned to stop at Chesterfield for a fortnight
more at the least and would be delighted to meet her
fiancé, who might find it in himself to soften little Alice's
heartache by autographing a portrait photograph for her.

If Audrey were to give me a telephone number, I might ring in a couple of days and propose that they both lunch with me?

Audrey hesitated a while before answering. She was evidently tempted to have Ronnie meet a fan as articulate as I was yet made ill-at-ease by the notion of confiding his whereabouts to someone who was after all a complete stranger and possibly also troubled by the implication latent in my request that she and her fiancé were living together.

It would, she said at long last, be better if I were to give her my number, so that she and Ronnie might call me when convenient.

Since her telephone number was already in my possession, it wasn't the withholding of it in itself that left me somewhat restless and disgruntled. Rather, it was the absence on her part of wholehearted confidence in my sincerity – an affront at which my pride revolted even while my conscience told me it was well deserved; it was the horror on my part at the thought of being compelled to wait, for who knew how long, for an incoming call; and (although this was the least of my concerns) the fact that I would have to admit being lodged in a motel and hence also have to explain away the groceries I carried under my arm. But when I handed her the card that the proprietress of the motel had given me, in the event of my failing to remember the address, Audrey treated it to a quite brief and inattentive glance before putting it in her purse and appeared unaware of any inconsistency in the situation. Then we shook hands again and went our separate ways.

★

Waiting is not a passive activity. It consumes, it devours, it pitilessly spews out one's every hour, minute, second; it deters one from setting about the very meanest of quotidian chores; one comes to feel that the worst of the afterlife's eternal damnation must be the sheer eternity of it and not the damnation. I shall not keep the reader waiting as I was kept waiting by Ronnie.

After five days which passed for me as in a dream, as in the kind of discontinuous dream-cycle during which a sleeper remains half-alert, half-capable of assimilating his flushed and fevered state to the reality of his waking hours, five days of pacing the length and breadth of the drab and narrow confines of my sitting-room and, ultimately, of not daring to emerge from it at all for fear the call be put through in my absence, of however brief the duration, the telephone rang. I let it ring twice, then picked up the receiver.

It was Audrey's voice that I heard. She wondered, first of all, whether I remembered meeting her. Whether I remembered meeting her! – I almost had to cup my hand over the mouthpiece, so powerful was the urge to scream out at the autism that seemed for ever to separate me from the world. She apologised for her tardiness in calling me back and finally said that, if I were free that very evening and had no objection to 'taking pot luck', Ronnie and she would love to have me to dinner. Anxious not to let my voice betray by a mere tremor the elation I felt at this turn of events, I replied that it would be my pleasure. I made as though I were methodically noting down an address I already knew, lent an ear to Audrey's detailed instructions as to how I should proceed to Jefferson Hill and promised to be there at seven.

The remainder of that same afternoon I spent at the town's hairdressing salon, where my hair was trimmed and my nails finely manicured by an obsequious little fusspot of a man who, with his own elaborately crimped and wavy locks, was the very image of a barber in a French farce; in the more expensive of its two men's shops in search of a 'stylish' silk tie that might set off to advantage the pale grey, slim-waisted suit I had not yet worn in Chesterfield as it had been bought and laid aside for exactly the present occasion; then in a chic and overwhelmingly fragrant flower shop – located, possibly as a result of someone's drolly irreverent sense of cause and effect, next door to the gun store – where I purchased a vast bouquet of white 'long-stemmed' roses. Yet, with all that to do, I found myself, at about five-thirty, back in the motel room, bathed, shaved and dressed, condemned to another nervous but now also deliciously tantalising hour or so of pacing back and forth.

I set off for Jefferson Hill at precisely six thirty-five, walked at a steady pace through the still fairly animated streets and made my way where the township itself started to thin out. At six fifty-five I stood on the doorstep of no. 16. I took a deep breath and rang the bell.

It was Ronnie who opened the door, Ronnie whose voice I had already heard coming from within the house – half heard, rather, against a background of crashingly loud music – calling out, '*I'll* get it.' He was barefoot and had on a pair of faded jeans and a plum-red V-neck sweater over a blue-and-green checked shirt. That these colours did not produce a very elegant effect together I scarcely noticed: it was as though, having waited so long for this moment, I were now standing face to face with nothing short of a myth, with at the very least some dashing, dazzling product of man's imagination, a Romeo, a Fabrizio, a Steerforth.

Smiling winningly, a casual, open smile, the most elementary of social graces, which I nevertheless thrilled to as though it heralded a declaration of love, he extended his hand.

'Hi. You must be Giles.'

I took Ronnie's hand in my own, my flesh enfolded his, so long desired. Then he said, nodding his head backward in the direction of the music, 'Are you into heavy metal?'

Weeks of poring over magazines destined for fourteen-year-olds having familiarised me with that curious expression, I would have been quite capable of parrying the question without making a fool of myself in the other's eyes. But before I could answer, Ronnie himself, with nothing but sweet amiability in his manner, added, 'No, I guess not.' Then, with a sideways switch of his arm, 'Come in, come in. I'll turn it off.'

Everything else he said, as I accompanied him along a narrow hallway and into a bright, high-ceilinged living-room, was just as banal – 'Honey, Giles is here' (this to his fiancée, who was presumably in the kitchen) or 'Let me take your coat' or 'Audrey, come see the flowers Giles brought you' – but to his lover's ear they became so many mingled harmonies. And I longed to kiss the two pearly, slightly rabbity front teeth I had come to know as well as my own.

The room, which also contained a dining table, already laid, had been done more tastefully than might have been expected, but what my eye was drawn to were those objects alone, recalled from a hundred photographs, which had become the very fetishes of my passion. A soft toy panda sitting comically at the fireside; an ornately painted guitar propped up in a corner; a silver-framed snapshot on the mantelpiece of a very long-haired Ronnie standing shoulder to shoulder with the singer Bruce Springsteen, inscribed *To R. B. from the Boss*; a tiny Japanese bonsai tree in a pot.

Audrey stepped in from the kitchen wiping her hands on a tea-towel, reminding me with a simper that I had agreed to take pot luck and leaving again almost at once to find a vase for the gratefully acknowledged white roses. Ronnie offered me a drink – apologising because there was nothing in the house but beer and club soda – and our first evening together got under way.

The conversation began with an exchange of those inoffensive commonplaces that characterise all tentative social communication – bland generalities about Britain and the United States, about how uninhabitable the Hamptons had become of late, especially on summer weekends when the influx of New Yorkers fleeing the humid metropolis made it next to impossible to find a parking space or a half-decent table in a restaurant – and we even heard ourselves edifying each other with brief and nuggety profundities about the weather and the likeliest effect upon it of the damage done to the ozone layer. With the unembarrassed candour that I might have expected of him, however, and that could only honour him the more in my eyes, Ronnie soon showed himself impatient to have me speak of his career; and that evening I talked to the young actor as I am certain

no one had ever talked to him before nor, am I equally
certain, would ever again. I proceeded to detail his
performances scene by scene, almost shot by shot, as
though blessed with some sort of infallible photographic
memory. Ronnie, unable to contain his delight at hearing
himself spoken of with such authority and expertise, his
eyes aglitter, his two elbows poised on the table top, his
bare, suntanned arms converging at hands tightly clasped
under his chin to form the apex of a triangle that
bewitched me just to look at it, ingested what I was
saying not merely with his mind but with his entire body
and seemed to catch his breath again and again in
incredulous fascination as I complimented him on this
minor piece of business or that line of dialogue that had
been delivered, as I would suggest, with an unsuspected
poignancy of tone and expression. And, as I spoke,
Audrey would turn to him again and again with a glow
of pride and satisfaction on her face that I was gratified
to interpret as meaning, 'Didn't I tell you? Didn't I tell
you?'

Watching the spellbound youth opposite me at table,
with the tiny bonsai tree on a wall-shelf behind his head,
it struck me just how like that tree Ronnie himself was,
a slim, exotic stem of flesh all of whose tender shoots
ought to be so pampered, so lovingly nurtured, all the
deadwood in him so tidily trimmed off, that he too would
come to see, as his lover did, that it would be better were
he never to grow up at all. I did not doubt that I had
wholly captivated him, on whose features admiration
was now freely commingling with a certain awe and a
respect for age and experience that was perhaps something new in his life; and this was confirmed by a trivial

but for me momentous incident that occurred towards the end of the evening. It happened that, while I was in full flight, Audrey had interrupted to ask whether or not I would take coffee and, to my great and secret gladness, Ronnie replied so snappishly to her that she had stalked off into the kitchen in a sulk. Nor did he follow her to ask forgiveness, merely shrugging his shoulders and raising his eyebrows at me as though to say, 'Women!' It's true that, on her return to the living-room with the coffee, he now slightly shamefacedly made her sit by his side on the sofa, pecked her affectionately on the cheek and sat for a long while afterwards with his arm encircling her neck; yet such an obviously dutiful and deliberately public display of endearment did not, could not, dampen my intoxication at the involuntary fit of impatience that had preceded it.

Nothing had been said all evening of the precise nature of Ronnie's relationship with Audrey. But, shortly before midnight, when I stood on the doorstep saying goodbye, and was on the point of proposing that we dine again but next time at my invitation, Ronnie, thanking me over and over for my words of advice and shaking my hand for the longest time, also happened to announce in that casual way he had that, because of an imminent writers' strike, the shoot of his new film had been brought forward by several weeks and Audrey and he would be flying out to Hollywood five days hence to be married there instead of on Long Island as initially planned.

I offered the young couple my very best wishes and turned away from the house on Jefferson Hill as though entrusted with a fatal gift. As I slowly walked down towards the town, in which only a few stray house-lights still flickered in the darkness, each of them, as I fancied, separated from its closest neighbour by millions of light years, my brain seethed in uncontrollable ebullition, the richest expectations mixed with quite unbridled despair. I *had* set out to conquer the boy and I *had* conquered him, filled his puppyish mind with ambitions and aspirations such as it could never have entertained on its own, such, too, as his foolish little dormouse of a fiancée would never have been able to inspire. I could not lose him now.

Fretful with longing, I didn't sleep at all that night, and the whole of the next day just seemed to prolong the same, almost hallucinatory state of mind. The following night, too, I battled with every species of conflicting desire, and it was only in the cold light of the second morning that I knew a quick decision was in place.

Exactly at ten o'clock I dialled the actor's number – that number which by rights I ought not to have known. It rang seven times before it was answered, dozily, by Ronnie himself. With a thickly voiced apology, he asked to absent himself again and the telephone stayed dead for a minute or two. When he returned, he sounded fresher and more alert, as though he had sprinkled water into his eyes. I apologised in my turn, for having wakened him, then put it to him that he and I might meet that morning in town. Ronnie was clearly surprised, even startled, by my invitation and questioned me on its purpose. And when I insisted that he must wait until he see me for an explanation, he chided me for being so mysterious with what he charmingly called 'an old friend' but agreed to meet me a half-hour later. Where? I remembered that in Irving's there were one or two rather isolated and private booths at the back that would most probably remain unoccupied until the lunch-hour rush and allow us to converse undisturbed. Ronnie fell in with the suggestion and we hung up simultaneously. Neither of us had made mention of Audrey.

He was, as I had known he would be, late – fifteen minutes late. I had selected the very furthest booth from the entrance of the diner, one that was nevertheless directly in its view. There I ordered a coffee and sat quite patiently stirring the spoon and staring out ahead of me. And even if Ronnie was late, he was the first customer to arrive after I had myself. He sauntered in from the street, turned out in his eternal blue jeans and a thin linen jacket, the collar upturned, the cuffs of the sleeves folded back over his wrists, still his unmistakable, ravishing self, in spite of a pair of dark glasses that lent him a somewhat rakehell air. He slouched down opposite me, ordered a Coke, pushed the glasses up on to his lovely head of blond hair and quizzically cocked his sun-kindled features.

Irving's hoarse-voiced chatter was audible at the far end of the restaurant; a single customer perched on one of the barside stools was monotonously tapping a spoon against a saucer as he turned the pages of a newspaper; there could be heard, too, from beyond the half-open door to the kitchen the orgasmic crescendo of a racecourse commentary. When I started to speak, in a rush of words, I was quickly made aware that I was merely reiterating the compliments I had paid Ronnie the previous evening; so that he, if just as visibly gladdened as he had been, if smiling that same bashful smile of his, also looked a little baffled, as though he could not quite comprehend why he had so soon been called out to hear them again.

It was then that I adopted the loftiest overview imaginable, that I spoke to the unlettered boy of the Oedipus and of Oedipal themes, of that now tender, now torturing, imbroglio of love and hate, of a love near to hatred and a hatred nearly indistinguishable from love, wherein fathers and sons have eternally ensnared each other, of the related theme of the quest for law and authority, a theme that could be traced through the entire history of the world's drama, from the prototypical and emblematic personage of Oedipus himself to that, his counterpart of a more contemporary psychology, of Hamlet. I then passed on to the theme's resurgence in the American theatre of our own century and the pervasive influence that such a resurgence had had on the modern American cinema; and if, there, I was very much less sure of my thesis, was in truth half improvising, it thrilled me that Ronnie would nod his head and mutely spur me on, as though we two were as father and son ourselves. These, I concluded, and not the roles unworthy of him that he had hitherto been assigned, and that if they were not to become stumbling blocks must be considered as mere stepping stones, these were the roles upon which he was born to leave his mark, roles whose dominant mythology was that of the father, of the search for the father and the death of the father, narratives of a true Oedipal inspiration.

Then, tensely excited, finding that I had often to clear my throat, growing incredulous myself at what I was saying, I took a more personal and intimate tack, I insinuated – none too subtly, I fear – that the youth's career, possibly his very life, was reaching a turning point and that he would regret it ever after were he to be tempted down the wrong path. I was mortified to hear myself all but wheedling in my endeavours to make him understand that he should not lazily fly out to Hollywood and make *Hotpants College III* as though there were no alternative – that an alternative did indeed exist.

It was towards the close of this speech that I first noticed Ronnie shifting uneasily in his seat and, once or twice, when my voice seemed to become painfully shrill, turning his head to make certain we were not overheard. But, only a moment later, his face would crease into a smile again, he would shrug his shoulders and with a half-humorous pout of self-deprecation seek to make light of his discomfiture; and, when he spoke, he would try to intimate that everything he had heard me say, now and three days earlier, represented little more for him than, as he put it, 'a terrific ego trip', to be luxuriantly savoured, to be positively lapped up, not to be taken really seriously for a second.

Yet the vulnerable young creature was, I believed, already half inside the trap I was setting for him; I could read in his eyes how he still craved to gorge on the praise and attention the inadequacies of his career had hitherto denied him; and although I could not afford to have him too alarmed, the course to which I had committed myself was irreversible and there was nothing for me now but to press home what I felt to be my advantage. Thus I reminded him that I was a writer, that, even if he had not heard of me, I was, in England, in Europe, a famous writer, esteemed, respected, paid attention to. And I vowed, I vowed that I would henceforth devote myself to his career, that I would write the kind of role and the kind of film which his gifts merited, that I was ready to subordinate everything else in my life to that end – it would be a total commitment on my part and it would demand no less total a commitment from him. 'I realise,' I added, and God knows what had got into me, 'that you are bound by temporary attachments – ' and as I said these fatal words I waved my arm in vaguely the direction of Jefferson Hill.

Ronnie would not now suffer me to go on. 'Temporary attachments?' he repeated in disbelief. He shook his head as though believing I was insane or else merely beneath contempt, and there began to appear on his face an expression of tight-lipped cynicism such as I had never seen in any of his photographs.

All the more desperately did I struggle to reanimate the eloquence, the glib command, which had served me well until then. I attempted to evoke, to set forth in words that he wouldn't misunderstand, the type of relationship that had ever existed between a younger man and his elder, this elder being a writer, oftentimes a poet, by whom the youth would accept to be moulded, shaped, educated, inspired on to heights of spiritual and intellectual endeavour he could not, could never, attain by himself. In years past, I told him, there had arisen almost a tradition of such romantic friendships, and I mentioned Cocteau and Radiguet, Verlaine and Rimbaud –

My allusion to Rimbaud seeming in particular to confuse him, I don't know why, I unguardedly hastened to explain it and made my second fatally wrong move – 'Rimbaud,' I said, 'the French poet, who was Verlaine's lover.'

With a swift, anxious glance over his shoulder, Ronnie drew his dark glasses back down on to his eyes, their two blind man's sockets making his face appear rather paler than perhaps it was. He made to speak, as though disgustedly to repudiate my advances, then seemed to soften again. With a gentle, graceful flick of his wrist he took my hand in his, and for one brief, blissful instant I imagined, but no, it was only to shake it, politely and coldly – the brisk, neutral handshake of someone on the point of taking his leave.

He started to rise to his feet, thanked me for what I had said about his work and hoped that he could nevertheless continue to believe that I had been sincere. It was all over, as I knew, yet I cared for nothing but to keep him for as long as possible at my side, before my eyes, where I could simply look at his face and listen to his voice. And when, because of the width of the table and narrowness of the booth, he had to edge out sideways, I found myself madly clinging to his wrist, to his hand, holding him back and then, in a fierce whisper, forcing from myself the inevitable, irreplaceable words, hackneyed and sacred: 'I love you!'

Standing quite erect now, Ronnie pulled my hand from his, he peeled it off, rather, finger by finger, as he might have removed one of his own gloves, he turned his jacket collar up so that it half-concealed his face and without addressing another word to me strode out of the restaurant.

Once more alone in the booth, I let my head sink into the palms of my cupped hands. I felt a slight viscousness on the tip of one finger and realised to my horror that a little bubble of snot had been blown out of one of my nostrils.

'Dear God,' I said to myself, 'what have I done?'

★

It was late when I reached the motel, too late in any event for me to think of returning the same day to New York. I advised the proprietress, who greeted the news almost as though it were her own personal misfortune, that unforeseen circumstances obliged me to leave early next morning and paid my bill in advance. I also made a request – an uncommon one, it appeared, for such a modest establishment – for writing paper, an envelope and stamp.

Having made my luggage ready against the morning, I spent that same evening writing a long letter to Ronnie; just before midnight, I walked for the last time into the centre of town to post it. Unless the postal system were super-naturally efficient, it would not, I was sure, be delivered to the house on Jefferson Hill until after I had entirely removed myself from Chesterfield.

Later still, in my little bungalow sitting-room, illuminated only from without by the motel's neon sign, I gave myself up to my thoughts.

I thought of how my lover would receive the letter; how abnormally solemn he would become when he read it; how, too, he would certainly decide to keep its nature and contents from his fiancée, doubtless the first secret kept from her in a union that would know many others; and how, at the last, he would briefly toy with the idea of destroying it. But if I knew him, and no one on earth knew Ronnie Bostock better than I, he would not destroy it. Rather – in a fuller and more mature understanding of what had happened to him and equally of what might have happened to him, in the slow dawning on him that his career and his life, boding so far from brilliantly either of them, might have taken a very different course

137

had he but been capable of opening his heart to another whose own life he would soon see to have been transformed and perhaps even cut off in its prime for love for him – he would return to it often, read it again and again over the years, then no longer have to read what he would have come to know by heart but cherish it against the insentient world as a source of pride both possessive and possessed. And because he would not destroy it, it would end by utterly destroying him.